NIGHT AT THE MUSEUM

A Junior Novelization

NIGHT AT THE MUSEUM

A Junior Novelization

Written by
Leslie Goldman

Screen Story and Screenplay by
Thomas Lennon & Robert Ben Garant

BARRON'S

Written by Leslie Goldman
Screen Story and Screenplay by Thomas Lennon & Robert Ben Garant
Based on *The Night at the Museum* by Milan Trenc (Barron's
Educational Series, Inc., 1993, 2007)

All inquiries should be addressed to:
Barron's Educational Series, Inc.
250 Wireless Boulevard
Hauppauge, New York 11788
www.barronseduc.com

Library of Congress Control No.: 2006022019

ISBN-13: 978-0-7641-3576-7
ISBN-10: 0-7641-3576-7

Library of Congress Cataloging-in-Publication Data
  Goldman, Leslie.
    Night at the museum : a junior novelization / written by Leslie
  Goldman; based on the motion picture screen story and screenplay
  by Thomas Lennon and Robert Ben Garant.
      p. cm.
    ISBN-13: 978-0-7641-3576-7
    ISBN-10: 0-7641-3576-7
    I. Lennon, Thomas. II. Garant, Robert Ben, 1970-   .
    III. Night at the museum (Motion picture) IV. Title.
    PZ7.G5686Nig 2006
                                                    2006022019

PRINTED IN THE UNITED STATES OF AMERICA
9 8 7 6 5 4 3 2 1

CHAPTER 1

L arry Daley was having a bad day. Lately, he'd been having a string of bad days. They added up to not just a bad week or a bad month, but actually, a fairly bad few years. Yet, today was even worse than usual. Today, they'd shut off his cable.

Larry hadn't paid the bill, but was that any reason to deny him television? He didn't think so, which is why he called the cable company to try and reason with them.

"Hello, Delores, this is Larry Daley. You guys shut off my cable yesterday. I know the bill is late, but we've just had some minor organizational problems over here."

Larry was stretching the truth. His problems were major, not minor. He wasn't organized in the slightest. His apartment was a huge mess. It was filled with a jumble of books and papers, hockey equipment, and boxes. One look at his apartment and a person would think he'd either just moved in or was about to move out. In fact, neither was the case. Larry was just a big slob.

As he pleaded with the cable lady, he paced back and forth in the small living room. When he walked past his latest invention, The Snapper, he glanced at it. The front of the box showed an old woman with a big smile on her face, snapping her fingers to light up a room. You've heard of The Clapper? Well, that was a successful invention. The Snapper, which Larry invented? Not so much.... Of course, that was small potatoes compared to his other failures.

"The thing is," said Larry, "I've got my son staying with me tonight and we were gonna watch the Rangers game, but if there's no cable, I mean it would really...I'd just hate to disappoint him. I've already mailed the check. So, can you please turn it back on?"

Larry pulled back the dingy curtain that led to his son Nicky's room. It was the best-looking part of the whole apartment. The walls were freshly painted and hockey posters hung from them, neatly. The bed was made. The shelves were stocked with board games and model jets. Larry was always careful to make sure that Nicky's room didn't get messy. Mostly, he did this by staying out of the room when Nicky wasn't around. For some reason, it seemed like whatever Larry went near turned into a disaster.

Yet, perhaps his luck was about to change. It sounded like the cable lady was actually buying his story.

"Oh, that's great. Thank you so much, Delores. You're the best. Good-bye."

Larry hung up the phone and realized he was late for a very important appointment. He grabbed a folder from his desk. Inside were the plans for his latest business idea. He wanted to open up a restaurant called *The Daley Grill: An International Dining Experience*.

Larry checked himself out in the mirror. He smoothed down his dark brown hair. He flashed his pearly white teeth. In jeans and his best button-down shirt, he was looking good. Larry put his folder in his bag and headed to his meeting.

No way could this go wrong.

As he headed to his car someone called his name. "Larry?"

Turning around, Larry found himself face-to-face with Miguel, his super. "Hey, Miguel. Como estás? You get that CD I burned you?" Larry asked.

"Yeah, man, I like it," said Miguel. "Thanks."

"Good. I thought you'd be into the Gipsy Kings. All right, I've got to run."

Larry hoped to make a clean escape, but Miguel had some unfinished business with him.

"I need the rent, Larry."

Larry stopped short. He was so close to getting away. Turning around slowly, he decided to play dumb. "I didn't give it to you?" he asked.

Miguel wasn't falling for it. They both knew that Larry hadn't given him the rent check. "You're two months late," said Miguel. "If I don't have it by January 1, I've got no choice but to evict you. I'm sorry."

Larry wasn't worried. He'd been late with the rent plenty of times. Of course, he'd also been evicted plenty of times.

"Don't worry. You'll have it. I'm about to close on a major deal. Cash flow is not gonna be a problem," Larry promised. "See you later, Miguel."

Larry hopped into his old heap of a car and started it up. He was hoping to make it out of there before his landlord could argue with him.

"January 1, Larry. Two weeks," Miguel called.

"Got it," said Larry. What he was really thinking was, I hope I'll have it.

Larry sped to his meeting. It was in SoHo in downtown New York. He was running a little late, but luckily he found a great parking spot in front of his soon-to-be restaurant.

At the moment, it was a dingy, vacant storefront, but Larry had vision. He had imagination. All he needed was the money.

After climbing out of his car, he placed a brown paper bag over the parking meter. Scrawled on the bag were the words "Broken Meter." This was a great way for Larry to get out of wasting change to pay for parking.

Soon he was giving his three potential investors a tour of the place. "If you'll turn to page one of your business plan," Larry said, trying to sound as official as possible, "you'll find the basic layout of the restaurant."

The men opened up their folders to the first page. This wasn't exactly hard to do, because besides the cover, there *was* only one page in the business plan.

Larry explained what he thought was a brilliant plan, a sure moneymaker, and probably his best idea, yet. "We're going to go for an Asian fusion sort of thing," he said confidently. "There will be a sushi bar around the perimeter. Six shabu-shabu stations in the center here."

"Shabu-shabu?" asked one of the men. "We're dentists, Larry. Talk to us in English."

Larry said, "You sit around a pit of boiling water and cook your own food. It's very big in Japan."

The second man nodded, thinking about this. "Interactive dining. I like it. This is an interesting investment opportunity."

"I don't think we can go wrong," said Larry, clearly pleased.

"What are you looking at in terms of food cost to profit ratio?" asked the first man.

"Uh, it's... it'll be..." Larry was afraid the questions would get complicated. To be honest, he hadn't done all that much research into the financials of the business. Why waste his time crunching numbers? There was no need. He knew—he just knew that it would be a huge success. "High yield. Very solid ratio," Larry assured them.

"Can we meet the chef?" asked the third man.

Details, details, thought Larry. What is it with these guys?

"Yeah, I'm actually looking into a few guys. That won't be a problem. There are a lot of great cooks in New York."

"Who know how to do shabu-shabu?" asked the third man.

"The thing is, you really cook it yourself, so..." Larry was starting to get nervous. Actually, he didn't have anything else to say on the matter. It seemed as if they were losing interest. This had happened before, with other investors. It baffled Larry. How could these guys *not* want to give him the money, when his plan was so brilliant?

The second dentist took a closer look at the business plan. "I don't see your résumé in here. You've worked at other restaurants in the city?"

"Yes," said Larry. "I've actually held several managerial positions, in neighboring fields."

Last fall, Larry had been fired from Kinko's, which was next door to a great little Italian restaurant. This is what he meant when he said "neighboring," but he decided not to share that part.

"So you've never worked in a restaurant?" asked the third man.

"No. But that's a minor detail," said Larry. "I'll be the big-picture guy. I'll run the front of the house. We'll hire people to handle the rest."

The three dentists exchanged skeptical looks. The problem with Larry's plan was, well, it wasn't exactly planned out. One of them handed his folder back to Larry.

"You know what, gentlemen. I'm going to pass," he said.

"No, why?" asked Larry. "This is gonna be great. We'll open the first one, then we think about franchising."

The third man glanced at his watch. "I've got to run, too," he said. "I have a root canal at three o'clock."

"Sorry, Larry," said the first man. "I'll see you at your next cleaning. Keep flossing!"

As they walked away, Larry stood there, holding his three folders. That didn't go well at all. How was he going to pay his rent in two weeks? He didn't know but decided to look on the bright side. At least he'd managed to get the cable turned back on.

Walking back to his car, he had a funny feeling in his gut. Something wasn't right. He pulled the brown paper bag off the meter. Someone had crossed out the words "Broken Meter" and written below, "Nice Try."

There was a ticket on his windshield. Worse than that: A big orange boot was wrapped around Larry's back tire.

"No, no!" Larry shouted. He kicked the boot and then yelped, as the pain shot up his leg. His big toe throbbed. That hurt. That hurt, a lot!

Then he noticed his watch. "Oh, crap," said Larry. Realizing there was no way to pry the boot off his car, he made a run for it.

An hour later, Larry jogged up to the entrance of his son Nicky's school. A teacher was up on a ladder about to take down a banner.

"Hey, Mike," said Larry as he caught his breath. "Have you seen Nicky?"

Mike smiled down at Larry. "Erica came by to pick him up. He was waiting a pretty long time."

"I know. I had..." Larry tried to swallow his guilt. "Car trouble," he finished. Just then he noticed what the banner said. "Welcome! Parent

Career Day!" This was the first he'd heard of it, which meant that Nicky failed to tell him. Was it on purpose, and just because he didn't actually have a career at the moment? Okay, so The Snapper hadn't worked. Yet Nicky didn't know about the restaurant failure, yet. It had to be because of The Snapper. Or perhaps it was because of the hundred or so other ideas that Larry had failed to make work.

"So today was, uh, Career Day?" asked Larry.

"Yeah," said Mike. "Nick didn't tell you?"

"Yeah, no, he did. I just...I must've forgotten. See you, Mike," said Larry. Although he forgot about many things (the rent, the cable bill, the electric bill), he definitely would've remembered Nicky's Career Day. Nicky was his only son. His best friend. His buddy.

Larry decided to go see Nicky at home. He lived with his mom, Erica, who was Larry's ex-wife. Now Erica lived with her fiancé, Don. They had a big fancy apartment on Fifth Avenue, in New York City.

"How's it going, Gabe?" Larry asked the doorman as he walked into the building's lobby.

"Not too bad, Larry," said Gabe. He picked up a small phone and rang up to the apartment.

"Mrs. Daley, your ex-husband is here."

Larry rode up in the elevator and knocked on the door. Erica let him inside. She already looked upset. "Hi," she said shortly.

Looking around, Larry realized that Erica's apartment was the exact opposite of his. It was enormous. It was clean. It had nice furniture. It had amazing views of the city. And it was paid for.

"I'm sorry, Erica," said Larry. "I was about to get him, but they put a boot on my car and—"

"You didn't pay your parking tickets?" asked Erica. She didn't sound surprised, which was kind of upsetting for Larry. It was almost like she expected him to fail. And was that fair? Just because he'd failed so many times before?

"No, the meter maid had it out for me," said Larry. "So...did Nick...not want me at Career Day?"

Erica sighed. "He's just a kid, Larry."

Just then Don walked into the room. As usual, he was dressed in a dark fancy suit. Attached to his belt were lots of gadgets—a cell phone, a BlackBerry, and a digital camera.

"There he is! Great to see you," Don said to Larry.

"Great to see you, too, Don," said Larry.

They shook hands. Both were quiet, after that, because they'd already run out of things to talk about.

"I'll go tell the little corn on the cob you're here," said Don as he headed down the hall.

"Your fiancé really manages to squeeze a lot of stuff onto that belt," Larry observed, totally innocently.

"Larry, stop it," said Erica.

"No, it's cool. He's like the Batman of stockbrokers," said Larry.

"Bond traders," Erica said. "He's a terrific guy and he loves your son. So, what's happening with the restaurant? Did you get your investors?"

"Yeah. No. Um, there were some problems. So I don't think it's going to happen. It's fine. I have other irons in the fire," said Larry.

"Uh-huh," said Erica.

Larry bristled. "'Uh-huh'?" he asked. "What does 'Uh-huh' mean?"

"Larry, come on, we've been through this a million times. When problems come up, you just seem to...bail," said Erica.

"I'm not bailing. I... opening a restaurant is very complicated. It just didn't work out." Rather than argue, Larry changed the subject. "You think Nick would like Queens? I might try to find a place out there. Little more space, maybe an above-ground pool."

"You're getting evicted again?" asked Erica. She'd heard this story before. She didn't want to hear it, again. "Larry, I don't know how much more of this Nick can take. Every few months you've got a new apartment, a new career. If Nicky wasn't involved, I wouldn't care, but this instability...it's bad for him."

"Well, I'm trying to figure things out," said Larry.

"I hope so, Larry. I'm just...I'm not sure Nick should stay with you until you get settled."

Larry felt his heart sink. Erica sure knew how to crush a guy.

"Really?" he asked sadly.

Erica frowned as she tried to explain. "He gets attached to one place, then in a couple of months, it's gone. It doesn't seem fair."

As Larry thought about this, he noticed Nick standing in the doorway.

"Hey, Dad," said Nick.

Seeing his son made Larry feel so much better. "Hey, buddy! You ready to carve it up?" he asked.

A little while later, they were in Wollman Rink in Central Park, at Nick's ice hockey game.

Nick skated toward the goal, pushing the puck forward. He glided across the ice quickly.

Larry cheered him on from the sidelines. "There you go, baby! Breakaway!" He was yelling more loudly than any of the other parents.

Nick pulled back his stick and took a slap shot. The puck went wide, missing the goal by a foot. Even worse, Nick lost his balance and fell.

Panicked, Larry ran out to the ice, slipping and sliding all the way over to his son.

"Nick? Nicky? You okay?" he screamed.

Nick was so embarrassed. "Dad, I'm fine. Will you get off the ice?"

Larry looked around. The game had stopped and everyone was watching him. Before he left, he leaned in close and whispered some advice. "Their left defenseman can't skate for crap. You work that side, you got an open shot to the goal."

Nick grinned at his dad. "Cool, thanks."

Larry looked out to Nick's teammates and said,

"As you were, skaters! We're good over here."

After he helped Nick stand up, Larry headed back to the sidelines.

Well, thought Larry, I may not be good at opening restaurants or inventing things or paying my bills, but at least I give good advice when it comes to Little League ice hockey. Too bad I can't turn *that* into a career!

Later that afternoon, Nick and Larry walked home through the park.

"You tore it up out there, dude. You keep working on that slap shot. I'm thinking the NHL is a serious possibility," said Larry.

"Yeah," said Nick. "I don't really want to be a hockey player anymore."

"All right, so what do you want to be?" asked Larry.

"A bond trader," Nick replied.

Larry looked at his son. He hoped Nick was kidding. Sadly, this didn't seem to be the case. "And where'd you get that idea?" he asked. "Reading bond trader comic books?"

"Don took me to his office on Wall Street last week," said Nick.

Larry nodded. "Uh-huh, that's cool. So, what? You want to dress up in a monkey suit and tie, sit in a cubicle all your life? Trust me, you can't play hockey in a cubicle."

"He's got a pretty big office," Nick said.

"That's not the point. I thought you loved hockey," said Larry.

"I still like it, but bond trading is my fallback," Nick explained.

"Your fallback?" Larry could hardly believe his ears. "You're too young to have a fallback. Where did you even hear that word?"

"Mom was talking to Don about all your different schemes."

"She called them schemes?" asked Larry.

"She said it was time you found a fallback." When Larry didn't respond, Nick asked, "Are you really moving again?"

"We'll see," said Larry. "There are some pretty cool places out in Queens."

"Isn't that kind of far?" Nick looked up at his dad. "I thought your restaurant is in the city."

"Yeah, that's on hold right now," said Larry. "But maybe I could open one out there."

Nick shrugged. He looked down at the ground and kicked a small rock. "I guess so."

It was obvious to both of them that Nick didn't believe his dad for a second.

"Hey," said Larry. "Hey, I want to tell you something. I know things have been kind of up and down lately, and that's been hard on you, but I feel like my moment is coming. There's something out there for me. Something great. And when I find it, everything is going to fall into place."

Nick looked up at his dad and asked, "What if you're wrong? What if you missed your moment and you're just an ordinary guy who should get a job?"

Larry knew that Nick didn't say this to be mean, but the words still stung.

"Yeah, well, we'll figure it out," said Larry. "Come on. I'll take you back to Mom's."

Larry thought about what his son said. Yes, it hurt, but Nick was right. Larry did need some sort of job. His rent was due and he didn't want to move, again.

Bright and early the next morning, Larry headed down to the employment office. He sat in a chair as Debbie, the lady working there, looked at his résumé. He tried not to squirm.

But it was hard. She seemed so judgmental.

"Mr. Daley, I can honestly say in forty-three years at this agency, I've never seen a résumé quite like yours," said Debbie.

Larry smiled widely and said, "Thank you."

"That wasn't a compliment," Debbie explained. "It says here you were the CEO of Snaptime Industries? You care to elaborate on that?"

"Yes, that was the umbrella corporation for my invention, The Snapper. You know, snap!" He snapped his fingers to demonstrate. "And the lights turn on. We sold about eight hundred units our first year of production."

"Didn't they already make that?" asked Debbie. She clapped twice.

Larry shook his head. This was a common mistake. "There is The Clapper, of course. That obviously stole a lot of our thunder. I personally never saw a big difference. I mean..." Larry clapped twice and then snapped. "Whatever. But I guess some people have trouble snapping."

"Clapping is easier," said Debbie. "You want to tell me why you got fired from Kinko's?"

"That was a little misunderstanding," said Larry.

Debbie squinted at the fine print in her folder. "My record says 'misdemeanor,' as in a crime."

"It was hardly a crime," said Larry. "The suits from corporate said we couldn't have Halloween decorations. Violated policy. Well, I'm not a suit, and all I did was carve out a couple of jack-o'-lanterns. Then boom, they fired me. I still say, you can't put a price on fun."

"Is that *all* that happened?" asked Debbie doubtfully.

Larry felt like it was getting very hot in the room. "The candle in one of them started making a lot of smoke, which set off the sprinklers. There was eighty thousand dollars worth of damage. So, I guess technically, you can put a price on fun. Apparently it's eighty thousand dollars. But the point is—"

"The point is, it's a week before Christmas and you're a college dropout with a criminal record and a résumé courtesy of the freak factory," said Debbie. "I can't help you."

"Debbie," said Larry. "Can I call you Debbie? Because I felt a connection when I entered this office and I think you did, too."

Debbie leveled her gaze at Larry. "I didn't feel a connection," she said coldly.

Larry wasn't ready to give up. "Debbie, I need a job... tomorrow. If I don't have one I... I just need it, okay? So I'm not begging you to find me something, but I'm pretty close to doing that."

Debbie sighed and looked through her files. "I might have one thing," she said, writing an address down on a card. "They've turned down everyone I've sent over, but who knows? You might get lucky."

"Great!" Larry said. Taking the card, he frowned down at the address. Then he looked back up at Debbie. "Do I have to wear a tie?" he asked.

CHAPTER 2

The next morning, Larry went to the Museum of Natural History for his job interview.

The museum was on Central Park West, across the street from Central Park. It was a grand and beautiful old building. As soon as he walked inside, he found himself face-to-face with a gigantic and ferocious-looking *Tyrannosaurus rex* skeleton on a riser. Because Larry didn't know where he was going, he headed for the information booth. There was a woman behind the desk. She was tall and pretty and busy typing on her laptop.

"Hey," said Larry. "Excuse me."

The woman didn't respond. She was too wrapped up in her work.

"Excuse me," Larry said, this time a little bit louder.

The woman looked up, startled. "Oh, I'm sorry," she said. "Can I help you?"

Larry nodded. "I'm here for a job interview with—"

But before he finished his sentence, the woman interrupted him. "Right, with Cecil Frederick. He should just be finishing his shift."

"I'm Larry Daley," said Larry.

"Rebecca Hutman," said the woman. She shook Larry's hand firmly. Rebecca was serious, all business. "I'm a docent here, a tour guide."

Larry looked around. "This place is amazing. I used to come here when I cut school. I'm a big-time history buff."

He pointed to a lifelike wax sculpture of Teddy Roosevelt on a horse. He held a sword in one hand and was pointing west with another. "There he is," said Larry, tapping the Teddy-sculpture's knee. "Teddy Roosevelt. One of the great..." Larry's voice trailed off. Who was Teddy Roosevelt? He wondered. And what did he do?

Rebecca waited, expectantly.

"One of the great mustachioed men in history," Larry finished.

Was this guy joking? Rebecca wondered. Didn't every grown-up know that Teddy Roosevelt was the president of the United States from 1901 to 1909? She wasn't impressed.

Neither was Dr. McPhee, who came racing toward Larry. "Do not touch the exhibits!" he bellowed.

"Sorry," said Larry, backing away.

Dr. McPhee turned his attention to Rebecca. "Ms. Hutman, we open in sixteen minutes," he said. "I cannot tolerate this chaos. This is a museum. It's not...I can't think of the proper analogy right now, but just get it together!"

"Will do, sir," said Rebecca.

As Dr. McPhee hurried off, Rebecca turned to Larry and said, "Dr. McPhee is the museum director."

"Huh, seems like a fun guy," said Larry.

Rebecca smiled. Finally! thought Larry. A smile!

"So, you'll find Mr. Frederick in the security office," Rebecca said.

"Okay. Where's that?" asked Larry.

"It's easy," said Rebecca. "Just go through the Hall of Civilizations and left through African Mammals. When you pass Attila the Hun, take the elevator to the basement. Once you're down there, it's three lefts and a right. Then straight. Then two more lefts."

Because Larry looked confused, Rebecca handed him a map. "Take this. Good luck, Mr. Daley," she said.

"Thank you," said Larry. He took off in the wrong direction.

Rebecca quickly corrected his mistake.

Eventually, Larry found his way to Cecil Frederick's office. Cecil was wearing a navy blue uniform. He was an old man, in his seventies, but he had lots of energy. He also seemed very friendly.

"Mr. Frederick?" asked Larry.

"Please, Mr. Frederick was my father. I'm Cecil. Glad to know you, Larry." Cecil offered his hand to shake. Once Larry shook it, Cecil added, "I like it. Good firm handshake. Says a lot about a man. Come in, come in."

The security office was shabby and dusty. A maze of boxes lined the floors. Filing cabinets were crowded against one another. It was a mess. And it smelled kind of moldy.

"I love your résumé, Larry. You're a very creative young man," said Cecil.

Larry beamed. Finally someone could appreciate his many talents! "I've tried to mix it up a little. Dabble in different fields," said Larry.

Cecil cut straight to the point. "Now, let's talk turkey. The museum is losing money hand over fist. I guess kids today don't care about a bunch of wax sculptures and stuffed animals. So, they're downsizing, which is code for firing, myself and the other two night guards."

"Wow, I'm sorry," said Larry.

"Eh, what can you do? We've been here forever. The director wants a new night guard. Someone younger," Cecil explained.

"Well, I'm pretty sure I can handle it," said Larry.

"Very well. Let me introduce you to my associates. Gus! Reginald!" he called.

Suddenly, Larry noticed that there were two old men sleeping in the corner of the office. One was short and stocky. The other was a little taller and more wrinkled. He hadn't seen them before because they were slumped down so much, they blended in with the file cabinets around them. Now their eyes popped open.

"Who is he?" asked Gus, the shorter one, as he glared at Larry suspiciously. "I'll beat him with my bare fists."

"Gus, this is Larry Daley. The kid who wants to be the new night guard."

Gus looked Larry up and down. He didn't seem impressed. "He looks like a weirdo," Gus said.

"Wonderful guard," Cecil said to Larry. "Terrible people skills."

"Hey, Gus. I'm Larry," said Larry.

Gus narrowed his eyes at Larry. "Don't try anything funny," he said.

"Gentlemen! We have a job candidate in our midst. He's got an excellent résumé and a winning attitude. I say we give him a shot," said Cecil.

"Let me ask you something, Meat Sauce. Can you follow instructions?" asked Gus.

"Uh, yeah," said Larry. "I'm a pretty good instruction follower."

"Then it's settled," said Cecil.

"Welcome to the night guards, Larry," said Reginald, holding out his hand.

Larry shook it. "All right. Thank you," he said.

"Meet me up on the second floor," said Cecil. "I'll throw on my orthopedics and give you a quick tour." Cecil stood up and then winced. He pointed to his leg, adding, "Arthritic knee. It's tough getting old, my friend."

Larry nodded as he left the room.

Once the guards were alone, they looked at one another.

"You really think he's the one?" asked Reginald.

"Oh yes," said Cecil. "He's the one."

Something strange was going on. These old guards were up to something fishy. Larry had no idea what it was, but he was about to find out.

A little while later, Cecil gave Larry a tour of the museum. First he showed him a room filled with tiny dioramas. Each one displayed a different scene from history, complete with miniature people and props. Larry peered at the Mayan Village diorama. Tiny men in loincloths held spears. They were surrounded by stone temples. Another diorama had a small coliseum with Roman gladiators and soldiers. Next to it was a scene from the Old West—cowboys on horses surrounded by Chinese and Irish railroad workers.

Larry was amazed at the detail. It all seemed so lifelike. Suddenly, everything went black. Someone had turned out the lights. It was too quiet. Larry felt the hairs on the back of his neck stand on end. He was kind of scared. Looking around he asked, "Cecil?" His voice wavered.

Once his eyes adjusted to the dark, he realized he was standing in front of a wax Attila the Hun. He was surrounded by a bunch of other Huns. Even though they were made of wax, they were so eerie looking. Larry had the chills.

Larry remembered studying Attila the Hun back in grade school. But his memories were a bit fuzzy. One thing remained clear. Attila the Hun had a reputation for being cruel, heartless, and violent. These warriors sure were fierce looking. And they seemed so real.

Larry wondered where Cecil could be. It seemed like the old guard just disappeared.

Suddenly, a sinister-looking medicine man jumped out from the shadows and grabbed onto Larry's arm.

Larry screamed.

Then the man moved the mask away. It was Cecil. "Oh, did I get you good!" Cecil laughed.

Larry was not amused. "Yup, that was a good one," he said.

"Seriously, though. No fooling around in here. This stuff is really old," said Cecil. "Moving on."

Cecil put the mask back on the medicine man and left the room. Before following, Larry paused to check out a giant stone head. Larry read the plaque next to the head. He learned that the giant head was a replica of the heads found on Easter Island in the South Pacific. The statues had been carved from volcanic ash. They stood more than twenty feet tall and weighed over twenty tons. The Easter Island heads were very mysterious. No one knew exactly where they came from or what their purpose was.

In the next room, Cecil pointed to the stuffed lions, elephants, zebras, and monkeys. "This, of course, is the African Mammals wing," he explained.

Larry moved forward so he could get a better look at the small monkey. "This guy is cute," he said, tickling the stuffed monkey's chin.

"We call him Dexter," said Cecil. "He's quite a little ball of fun."

Larry was confused. How could a stuffed monkey be a ball of fun? Before he could ask, Cecil had moved on.

Larry had to run to keep up with him.

"This is the Egyptian Hall," said Cecil.

In the middle of the room was a free-standing Egyptian temple. Statues of men with spears stood around the base of it. They were twenty feet tall and jackle-headed.

"This is the Temple of Pharaoh Ahkmenrah," Cecil explained. He shined his flashlight inside the temple, aiming at a large stone coffin. "That's the pharaoh himself. Died young. And that was his most prized possession." Cecil pointed at the gold tablet on the wall above the coffin. It was covered in hieroglyphics. "The Tablet of Ahkmenrah. It's 24-karat gold and it's worth a fortune."

"Very cool," said Larry.

Cecil smiled mischievously. "It is indeed very cool, Larry." There was more to the story, but Cecil didn't tell Larry. He didn't have to because Larry would find out the truth soon enough.

"Alrighty, then. Report here tomorrow at five, and we'll talk you through your duties," said Cecil.

Larry nodded. "I'll be here. Thanks."

As Cecil looked Larry up and down, he asked, "Oh, I almost forgot. What are you, about a 38 regular?"

"What do you mean?" asked Larry.

"Your jacket size," Cecil explained. "We need to fix you up with a uniform."

"You really think I need a uniform?" asked Larry. "I'll be the only one here. Who am I trying to impress, right?"

"You'll like the uniform, Larry," said Cecil. "Trust me. It gives you a sense of power."

Power, thought Larry. Why would I need that? Larry didn't ask Cecil. Clearly the old guy was hiding something. But Larry didn't think this was a big deal.

Later that night, Larry called up Erica, his ex-wife. "Tell Nicky we're not moving. I got a job at the Museum of Natural History."

"Oh, Larry, that's great," said Erica. "I'm so happy for you. This is good news."

"Thanks, Erica," said Larry. "Good night."

Larry could hardly wait for his first night on the job.

CHAPTER 3

The next day, Larry put on his uniform and went to work. He was happy to have a job, but the uniform sure was annoying. The jacket was itchy and the tie was too tight. He kept zipping and then unzipping his jacket. It looked bad no matter what he did.

Larry walked into the Museum of Natural History. It was so quiet, he could hear his footsteps echo down the empty hallway.

Soon he found himself face-to-face with the giant T-rex skeleton. It seemed as if the dinosaur was staring right through Larry.

Suddenly the lights went out. Larry whispered, "Cecil?"

Sensing something behind him, he turned around. All he could see was the ghostly glow of Cecil's head.

Larry screamed. Cecil laughed and the lights went back on. Turns out, Cecil was holding a flashlight under his chin so he'd look scary. The other two guards stood on either side of him. They thought the joke was pretty funny, too.

"I got you, Larry!" Cecil said.

"You scream like a woman," Gus pointed out.

"He did get you, son," Reginald added.

Larry was not so amused. "It's a great running joke you guys have going here," he said. He didn't mean it.

Cecil handed Larry a heavy ring of keys and a large flashlight. "Here are your keys and your torch," he said. "You'll want to strap those onto your belt."

"I'll just hold them," said Larry.

"Belt 'em up, hot dog," said Gus.

"Whatever you say, Gus," said Larry. When he put his keys on his belt he couldn't help but notice how heavy they were. He thought his uniform looked ugly before. Now it was even worse.

"Let's see. Keys, flashlight... I feel like I'm forgetting something," said Cecil. "Ah yes! The instruction manual." Cecil pulled a thick stack of legal paper out of his bag. It was stapled together, dog-eared and frayed. There were handwritten scribbles all over the cover and complicated-looking diagrams inside. Cecil handed it to Larry as if it were a precious, one-of-a-kind book.

"Larry, it is crucial you follow these instructions. Crucial," he said.

"Guys, come on," said Larry. He wondered if this were yet another joke. "I can walk around an empty museum holding a flashlight. It's gonna be okay."

"There's a little more to it than that, son," said Reginald.

Gus pointed to the manual. He was pretty serious. "Start at number one. Then number two. Then go to number three. Then—"

Larry interrupted. "Let me guess, number four."

"Are you cracking wise?" asked Gus. "Because I will sock you in your nose, tough guy."

"Leave him alone," said Reginald. "You got it covered, right, Larry?"

"I just follow the instructions," said Larry.

"Do them all. Do them in order. Do them quick. And the most important thing to remember is don't let anything in... or out," said Cecil.

Larry stared at him, wondering what he was talking about. This was a museum, after all. It wasn't a zoo!

"Good luck," said Cecil. He headed for the exit and said, "Moving on!"

All three of the old guards shuffled out the revolving door, leaving Larry all alone.

Once he was by himself, Larry sat down at the information desk and put the instruction manual in front of him. He leaned toward it, as if to begin reading. Instead, he decided to rest his head on it. It wasn't the most comfortable of pillows, but he'd definitely slept on worse.

Soon Larry was snoring so loudly, he woke himself up. He opened his eyes just in time to see a shiny blue beetle skitter across the floor.

It was strange looking, but Larry didn't think twice. Standing up, he stretched. Then he headed for the men's room. He had to cross the main lobby, where the T-rex skeleton should have been. Larry walked right past it, not even noticing that it had vanished.

As soon as he got into the men's room, he realized something was wrong. Larry went back outside. He did a double take. Still, no T-Rex skeleton.

But it couldn't have just disappeared. Larry walked closer. "Very funny, Cecil," he said.

"What are you, some kind of illusionist? You doing a David Copperfield trick here?"

Larry climbed up on top of the riser and waved his hands through the air where the skeleton should have been. He didn't feel a thing because it wasn't there.

"Okay, this is weird," said Larry.

Hearing the sound of running water in the distance, Larry got off the riser and walked to the end of the hall. He turned on his flashlight, rounded the corner, and flashed it on the water fountain.

The T-rex skeleton was bent over the fountain, getting a drink of water!

Because it was a skeleton, the water went into its mouth and through its body, spilling onto the floor. Of course, that wasn't the weirdest part. The weirdest part was, the dinosaur bones seemed alive.

Larry dropped his flashlight in shock. The clattering noise got the T-rex's attention. It stopped drinking and turned toward Larry.

Terrified, Larry felt his knees go weak. He backed away, holding up his hands and hoping the T-rex was a nice dinosaur.

Suddenly, the T-rex started running toward him.

"Holy crap!" yelled Larry, turning around and

scrambling out of the room. T-rex followed close at his heels.

When Larry made it through the room, the T-rex hit its head on the door and its skull fell off.

Larry dashed into the main lobby and tried to make his way through the revolving doors. "Come on. Revolve. Revolve!" he shouted. No matter how hard he slammed his body against the doors, they wouldn't move. He was locked in!

Meanwhile, T-rex was putting his skull back on his neck.

Larry dove behind the information desk. He reached up and pulled down the phone so he could call Cecil.

"Hello?" asked Cecil, who was enjoying his retirement party safe in his apartment.

"Cecil, it's Larry Daley. The dinosaur... the dinosaur is alive! What is going on here? How do I get this walking pile of bones away from me?" Larry yelled.

"Did you read the instruction manual?" asked Cecil.

"Of course not!" Larry yelled. "No one reads instruction manuals. Just tell me what to do!"

"Read the instructions, Larry," said Cecil. "They explain everything. See you in the morning."

"Wait! Did you guys lock me in here?" asked Larry. "Hello?"

The line went dead. Cecil had hung up on him.

Larry poked his head out from behind the desk. He grabbed the instruction manual. As he did, T-rex noticed him from across the room and started galloping toward him.

Larry flipped open the cover and read instruction number one: Throw the bone.

"Throw the bone?" asked Larry. "What bone?"

Just as he asked the question, a huge dinosaur bone dropped onto the ground in front of Larry. A second later, the desk lifted high up in the air, leaving Larry completely exposed. The T-rex set down the desk and moved closer.

Larry grabbed the bone and suddenly T-rex stopped. The dinosaur watched the bone with great interest. Larry threw it as far as he could, and the T-rex ran after it.

Larry took off toward the front door, hoping to make his escape. The T-rex got there before him. He dropped the bone at Larry's feet and nudged it forward.

Suddenly, it dawned on Larry. T-rex wanted to play fetch. Larry picked up the bone and threw it in the other direction. As the T-rex turned around, his giant wagging tail slammed into Larry. Larry flew across the museum floor and landed in a heap at the other end of the room.

Just then, Larry heard a deafening roar. It seemed to be coming from the back of the museum.

Larry stood up and hurried to the instruction manual. "'Lock up the lions or they'll eat you,'" he read. His eyes grew wide. "Lions! What *is* this place?"

The roar sounded again. As Larry ran off in the direction of the noise, he muttered, "This is so not worth eleven-fifty an hour."

The commotion was coming from the African Mammals wing. As soon as Larry got there, he was amazed to find that all the stuffed creatures had come to life. Zebras grazed. Elephants lumbered around. The mighty lions stretched their limbs. On either side of the wing's entrance was an iron gate. Both were wide open. Holding the instructions firmly in his hands, Larry walked through, trying not to draw attention to himself. As gently as he could, he pulled the first gate closed. Unfortunately, the gate squeaked. Loudly. Larry stopped and peered over his shoulder. Every single animal was looking at him.

Just then the biggest lion in the room roared.

"Oh, boy!" Larry gulped and ran, making a mad dash through the plains. He raced past elephants, monkeys, and zebras alike. The lion was right at his heels. Luckily, Larry made it to the other side in time and closed the gate just before the lion made it through. This was the closest call, yet. Larry's heart pounded in his chest.

Larry read his third instruction. "'Number three. Double check your belt. The monkey probably stole your keys.'" What monkey? Larry wondered. Just then he noticed the monkey who was holding up the key ring and smiling widely.

"Oh no," said Larry. "Bad monkey! Bad monkey!"

The monkey actually looked upset.

"You're Dexter, right?" asked Larry, remembering when Cecil mentioned the ball of fun. "Come here, Dexter. Come to Papa. Hand Uncle Larry his little keysies. That's my hairy little buddy." Larry moved forward. He was close to getting his keys back. But when he bent down to grab them, the monkey bit his nose.

Larry screamed.

Screeching, the monkey jumped on his shoulder and started pounding Larry's head with his tiny hairy fists.

He couldn't get it off. And the lion was still roaring. Even though it was locked up, it was still so scary. This was very bad, indeed.

Eventually, Larry managed to rip the keys away from Dexter. He searched for the right one so he could finally lock the gate. "You're some little ball of fun," he said.

Once he found the correct key, he locked the door and then turned back to the instructions. "'Number four. Put the blinders on the horses.'" Larry looked around, completely confused. "Where are the horses?" he asked.

As Larry searched for them, he ran past a bronze sculpture of Christopher Columbus reading a map, clearly trying to find something.

"Hey, uh, Napoléon?" asked Larry. "You know where to find horses around here?"

Christopher Columbus turned to Larry, clearly insulted. "Napoléon?" he asked. "That guy comes up to my knee! I'm Christopher Columbus! I discovered your whole country, and this is the respect I get?"

Of course, Columbus said this all in Italian, which Larry did not understand.

"I'm sorry, I don't speak French," said Larry, backing away.

Soon he passed the giant Easter Island head.

"Hey, dum dum," called the statue. He had a deep voice, which echoed through the halls.

Larry turned around. "Me?" he asked.

"No, the other dum dum. You new, eh? You new dum dum. You gimme gum gum," said the statue.

Larry reached into his pocket. "I might have an old Altoid, but—"

"Me want gum, dum dum," the statue bellowed.

"Stop calling me dum dum," Larry said.

"It's fun calling you dum dum."

"I'm not dum dum. I just don't have any gum gum. And why am I even talking to you?" asked Larry.

Suddenly he heard crashing in the distance. "What is that?" he asked.

"Hun Hun," said the statue. "Dum dum."

"What?" asked Larry. "What's Hun Hun?"

Larry looked across the hall and noticed Attila and the other Huns slamming their weapons against the window that lead to the outside.

"Oh, Attila the Hun," said Larry. "Hold on a second."

Larry tried to act casual as he walked up to the Huns. "Excuse me, guys? I'm Larry Daley, the new night guard. Cut it out, okay?"

The Huns weren't so interested in listening to Larry. They kept right on pounding against the grate.

"Stop it!" Larry yelled. "You're not getting out, so let it go."

Attila the Hun started to scream. "I-goo-goo ba-ba-ga-ga!"

"Yeah, I don't know what that means," said Larry.

"You're in big trouble, dum dum. You better run run," said the Easter Island head.

"Why do I need to run run?" asked Larry.

Easter Island head didn't answer. He didn't need to because somehow Attila the Hun had managed to free himself from his display case. He raised his giant sword and charged after Larry.

"Later, dum dum," said the Easter Island head, as Larry ran past him.

When he made it to the elevator, he pushed the button. "Come on, come on," he said. When the elevator arrived, Larry got on and pressed the basement level button. As the doors closed, Attila the Hun brought his ax in between the doors and wedged them open. He started screaming in Mongolian. "Heagoogoo..."

Just then the elevator dropped. Attila's head smacked into the top of the elevator and then disappeared.

That was a close call!

Larry had a few moments to catch his breath. The other Huns must have taken the stairs, because once the elevator doors opened, they spotted him. Larry ran into the main hall. He passed by T-rex, which gave him a great idea.

Grabbing the bone, he waved it in front of T-rex, turning so that T-rex was between him and the Huns. Scared of the giant dinosaur, the Huns backed off.

Larry managed to escape into the Hall of American History. A stagecoach sat in the center of the room. The wax horses at the front of it bucked and whinnied. Larry quickly put the blinders on the horses as the instruction book told him.

Just then, he spotted something. It was the wax sculpture of the Shoshone Indian woman. She was with wax sculptures of two white men. The plaque underneath them said: "Lewis and Clark with Sacajawea, the Greatest Tracker in History."

Lewis and Clark were explorers. In 1803, after President Thomas Jefferson made the Louisiana Purchase, he hired Lewis and Clark to explore the area. They started traveling on the Missouri River. They were gone for twenty-eight months and covered more than eight thousand miles. Sacajawea was the young Shoshone Indian woman who worked as their interpreter and tracker. Not that Larry remembered learning this.

Walking up to the glassed-in display case, Larry asked, "How's it going?"

Sacajawea looked back at Lewis and Clark, who seemed to be bickering. She shrugged.

Just then the Huns ran by. Larry said, "I should get out of here."

Sacajawea waved good-bye. She looked sad. Larry backed away, unable to take his eyes off her. Until he tripped over something and fell down.

Larry got up. He found himself face-to-face with someone crouched in the high grass. It was a Union soldier from the Civil War exhibit. The image was extra-spooky because the soldier had no facial features. He was just a life-sized guy in a uniform with a faceless cloth head. He was also holding a musket with a bayonet attached.

Even though he had no mouth, the soldier shushed Larry.

"What are you shushing me for?" Larry wondered.

The Union soldier pointed at the Confederate soldier nearby. Soon the Confederate attacked, plunging his bayonet into the Union soldier's chest. Cotton stuffing went flying as the Union soldier collapsed. Larry realized he was in the middle of a battlefield. Soldiers surrounded him! He crawled away, reading his instructions as he went.

"'Go inside the Temple of Ahkmenrah and lock up the stone coffin.'" Larry looked around, with no idea where he was.

He opened the first door he came to. It led to the Hall of Ocean Life. Larry popped his head in and found a gigantic blue whale suspended from the ceiling. When the whale spotted Larry, he let out a deafening blast of whale song right at Larry. The sound blew Larry's hair back and made his ears ring.

He slammed the door and moved on.

Next, Larry passed a group of Neanderthals. They were trying to start a fire by banging rocks and wood.

"You guys know where to find the Temple of Ahkmenrah?" asked Larry.

All four Neanderthals pointed in a different direction.

Soon Larry ended up in the right place. The Egyptian Hall was dark and spooky. The Temple of Ahkmenrah was a gigantic gold pyramid-shaped thing. Enormous and threatening-looking stone soldiers guarded it. The entire place was lit up by a shaft of light that came from the golden tablet.

"Hello?" asked Larry. "Anybody alive in here?"

All was silent. Larry clicked on his flashlight and tiptoed closer. At the base of the display he spotted a small electric box with a keyhole. Larry reached for his keys, wondering why they had to lock up a guy who'd been dead for two thousand years.

Just then, something let out a horrible, bone-chilling scream.

Larry jammed his key into the box and a large piece of Plexiglas slammed down, sealing off the coffin and the priceless Tablet of Ahkmenrah. Larry let out a deep breath, glad that that task was over with.

Next he went back to the Hall of African Mammals. As he read his next instruction, Dexter, the monkey, grabbed his book.

"Give it back, Dexter! I am *not* going to ask you again."

Dexter laughed and began ripping the instructions to shreds. By the time Larry caught him, only one instruction remained. When Larry read it, he realized it wasn't even an entire instruction. All the scrap of paper said was: "To survive Attila, you must..." The rest was cut off.

"That is just perfect! You know what, Dexter, I don't need the instructions, because after tonight, I quit. Maybe the next night guard will be a poacher!"

Dexter gasped.

"That's right, you *should* be scared. Not everyone is an animal lover like Uncle Larry here."

Larry headed back to the diorama room. His uniform was wrinkled. His nerves were frazzled. In short, he was a mess. He could still hear Attila the Hun's rabid war cries. He quickly hid behind a bench, just in time. Attila and the Huns were in the room, babbling in their strange language. "I-goo-ga-bigooga..." They did say one thing in perfect English: "main hall!"

Attila pointed downstairs and the other Huns nodded. They all took off for the main staircase.

Once the coast was clear, Larry crawled out of his hiding place and sat down on a bench. He thought he could relax. He didn't notice that six tiny Mayan hunters wearing loincloths were creeping up to the bench he was sitting on. They came from the Mayan diorama. Each one was only a few inches tall. Too tiny to do Larry any harm. Or so he thought. "Okay, that's cool," said Larry, watching them approach.

Just then, one raised a blowgun to his lips and launched a dart. It landed on Larry's cheek, and it felt like a mosquito bite. "Ow! Hey! What are you doing?" asked Larry, as another dart hit his cheek. He pulled it out. It was the size of a splinter. His cheek felt tingly. Larry had a funny feeling about the arrow, so he tasted the tip of it. For some reason, it was sour. Just then, he noticed that the Mayans were dipping their dart tips into tiny pouches of powder.

"Wawa?" asked Larry. "Whawa you do-wing therw?" His speech was slurred. Whatever was on those darts was making him sleepy!

The Mayans continued shooting their poisoned darts at Larry. Each arrow numbed a small part of his face. Soon he couldn't feel a thing. His brain felt foggy.

He couldn't even speak anymore. Larry stood up but the darts kept coming. He stumbled. He couldn't get away fast enough. Looking down, he realized that some other Mayans had tied his feet together with some sort of vines. He tried to pull them apart but tripped and fell flat on the floor.

Larry landed in the American railroad diorama. He found himself face-to-face with a tiny cowboy on a tiny horse.

"Yeeh haw!" yelled a cowboy, whose name was Jedediah. He swung his lasso over his head. "Tie him, boys!"

A posse of tiny cowboys ran out on their horses. They shot pistols in the air and threw small ropes over Larry's body.

"Hey!" said Larry. He tried to look around, confused. He could barely move his head. The railroad workers sang as they hammered Larry's ropes into the ground with tiny spikes. "She'll be coming 'round the mountain when she comes. She'll be coming 'round the mountain when she comes..."

Soon Jedediah yelled, "Bring in the steel, boys!"

"The steel?" asked Larry. "What steel?"

Suddenly, Larry heard a high-pitched train whistle. He realized he was tied to a set of miniature railroad tracks.

"Hey, what are you doing? Help!" Larry yelled.

The train was getting closer and closer. Larry screamed, but no one made any attempt to rescue him.

The train sped closer. Soon it was just inches away. Larry squeezed his eyes shut tight. It was about to hit him.

CHAPTER 4

T he train headed straight for Larry and
crashed into his nose. It bumped off and
then tipped over, with its toy wheels
spinning. It didn't even leave a scratch. In fact,
Larry hardly felt it.

Gathering up all of his strength, he pulled
himself free. It turned out, this wasn't exactly
difficult. The ropes they'd used weren't much
stronger than thread. Larry broke them in a
second.

As Larry stood up, many of the tiny creatures
ran away in fear.

"The monster is escaping!" someone yelled.

The tiny Roman legion lined up in front of
Larry. "Prepare the catapults!" yelled Octavius,
their leader.

Jedediah yelled, "Hold your fire, Octavius. This
here giant is on our land."

"I'm not a giant," said Larry. "I'm really just average height."

"Silence!" yelled Octavius. "The Roman Empire knows no boundaries, Jedediah." He turned to his troops and said, "Defenders of Rome—"

"Don't do it," Jedediah warned.

Do what? wondered Larry.

"Unleash the weapons!" Octavius shouted.

The Roman legion discharged their catapults, and a wave of tiny flaming arrows and fireballs streaked across the room. Some of them stuck to Larry's uniform. The flames started to spread. Larry was on fire!

As he quickly patted out the tiny fires, a familiar-looking mustachioed man on a life-sized horse galloped up. The man reached for Larry and cried, "My hand, boy—take it!"

It was Teddy Roosevelt. Once Larry was behind him on the horse, they rode away. Teddy saved Larry from the small but fierce diorama people.

When they were in the main lobby, Larry jumped off the horse—and collapsed.

"They were so little," said Larry, out of breath and still very scared. "I didn't think..."

Teddy Roosevelt shook his head. "My dear boy, never underestimate the little people. It is the little people who make up great nations."

Larry was stunned. "Aren't you..."

"Theodore Roosevelt, the twenty-sixth president of the United States. Born in 1858. Died in 1919. At your service."

"I'm, uh, Larry Daley, the new night guard. Nice to meet you, Mr. President."

"Call me Teddy. Now, Lawrence, every good citizen must be willing and able to pull his own weight. Don't make me save you again, because I will not do it. You must pull yourself up by your own bootstraps."

"Right. Got it. Thank you." Larry nodded.

"Now, if you'll excuse me. It's almost dawn. The hunt is still afoot." Teddy Roosevelt saluted. Then he pulled his rifle from his saddlebag and directed his horse, Lucky, out of the hall.

Moments later, Teddy spotted a woolly mammoth in the distance. He raised his rifle and was about to shoot when Larry said, "Wait! Excuse me, mind if I ask you..."

Hearing noise behind him, the mammoth ran away.

"Sorry," said Larry.

"Quite all right, my boy. It's your first night," said Teddy. To the mammoth he shouted, "I'll get you yet, ancient behemoth! Mark my words!"

Teddy continued stalking the mammoth. Larry chased after him. "Hey, wait up!"

"You get one question, lad," said Teddy.

"Why? Is it like some kind of three-wishes deal?" asked Larry.

"No, it's that self-reliance is the key to a vigorous life. A man must reach inward to find his own answers. Now, how can I help you?" asked Teddy.

"Well, I don't quite know how to put this. And, seriously, please don't take this the wrong way, but isn't everything in this museum supposed to be, you know, *dead*?"

Teddy chuckled. "Follow me, Lawrence," he said, leading Larry back to the Egyptian Hall.

They stood in front of the Plexiglas wall containing the stone coffin. Larry shined his flashlight on the Tablet of Ahkmenrah above it. The fancy gold-engraved hieroglyphics glinted in the light.

Teddy explained what it was. "The Tablet of Ahkmenrah arrived here from the Nile Expedition in 1952. And on that night, everything in the museum came to life. It has every night since."

"So, *everything* in the museum comes to life *every* night?" asked Larry.

"Correct," said Teddy.

"And I'm supposed to do *what*?" Larry asked.

"You're the night watchman," Teddy reminded him. "It's a very important job at this museum."

Larry backed away from Teddy. He couldn't believe what he was hearing. "Okay, this is impossible," he said.

"Nothing is impossible, lad. If it can be dreamed, it can be done. Your job, my dear boy, is to keep everyone inside the museum. If the sun rises and any of us are outside, we turn to dust." Teddy glanced at his watch. "Now it's nearing five o'clock in the morning. I'll help you restore order tonight, but mark my words, this is the last time I'll ever do so. Is that clear?"

"The last time, yes," said Larry.

"Then let's ride!" Teddy said. He grabbed Larry, pulled him onto the horse, and they were off.

By the time the sun started rising over New York City, Larry and Teddy had secured most of the museum creatures. Larry went over his checklist out loud. "I locked the diorama boxes.

The Neanderthals seem good. Attila is still running around somewhere, but..." Just then Larry spotted Teddy. He was looking at Sacajawea through his binoculars.

"What are you looking at, Mr. President?" asked Larry.

Startled, Teddy dropped his binoculars. He seemed flustered. "Ah, I'm, uh, I'm tracking, dear boy. A man has got to track! It's a good thing for the heart and the mind. Five o'clock. Back to the old podium, I'm afraid. Welcome to the family. See you tomorrow night."

Teddy got back on his horse and trotted off toward his podium.

Larry followed him. "I gotta be honest, Teddy. I don't think I'm coming back. Even if I wanted to, which I don't, the monkey ate the instructions. I have no idea how to deal with the Huns..."

"Any fool can follow instructions," Teddy said with a scoff. "You need to follow your heart, son. That's the true mark of a man. Tell me, Lawrence, what did you do before you took this post? Did you give up on that as well?"

"Well, uh, I dabbled in various fields," Larry said feebly.

Teddy was not impressed. "Dabbling is a far cry from doing, lad. Lawrence, some men are born great. Others have greatness thrust upon them. For you, this is that very moment."

Larry nodded. Whatever, he thought. I just want to get out of here.

Teddy reached over and patted Larry hard on the back. Larry almost fell over.

Then Teddy rode back to his podium, jumped onto it, and froze.

Larry was amazed. He walked up to the statue, fascinated. Teddy was so still, so silent, so—

"Bully, ha ha!" yelled Teddy.

Larry jumped back, scared.

Teddy laughed and said, "I gotcha, dear boy!"

"You got me," Larry repeated. "Everyone is *always* getting me. Good night, Teddy."

Outside, the sun was shining bright. A beetle skittered toward the door of the museum. It tried to get inside, but the door was closed. Just then a beam of sunlight shined down and the beetle started to shake, then glow. Soon, all the color and life drained out of it. Moments later it turned into a tiny pile of dust.

An hour later, Cecil walked up the museum steps. He opened the front door and headed inside. Gus and Reginald were with him. They headed to the information desk and found the tattered remains of the instruction manual. All that was left was a scrap of paper.

"Attila must have ripped him to shreds," said Reginald.

"Ouch," said Gus.

"Let's take a moment," said Cecil.

All three guards bowed their heads. Then Larry crept up behind them and yelled, "Good morning!"

All three guards screamed with surprise.

"Don't do that!" yelled Cecil. He clutched his heart with both hands. "We're too old for surprises."

"I thought you guys love surprises. The way you're always sneaking up on me. Or, you know, how you 'surprised' me with the fact that, um, THIS WHOLE CRAZY MUSEUM COMES TO LIFE AT NIGHT!" screamed Larry.

"We wanted to tell you, Larry, but you never would have believed us," Cecil explained.

"Their left defenseman can't skate. Work that side for an open shot to the goal."

"Debbie, I need a job...tomorrow."

The imposing entrance to the Museum of Natural History in New York City.

"That's the pharaoh himself. Died young."

"Throw the bone?"

Larry reads the instructions.

"Anybody alive in here?"

Larry is tied down like Gulliver.

"Isn't everything in this museum supposed to be...you know, *dead?*"

"There's no way out, Dexter. Now give me the keys."

Out of the dust, a mummy, wrapped in dirty, worn linen, kicks and screams.

"I'm scared, Dad."

"It is very nice to meet you, Larry."

Larry introduces Rebecca to Sacajawea and Teddy Roosevelt.

"Besides, we were keeping an eye on you. If anything happened, we'd have been here in a flash," Reginald assured him.

"Really?" asked Larry.

"No, we were asleep at home," Reginald admitted.

That figures, thought Larry.

Cecil explained, "The point is, Larry, we all sensed something special in you when you walked into our offices."

"Those two were sleeping," Larry reminded him.

Cecil decided to ignore that. "Any guy with a uniform and a flashlight can watch over a museum," he said. "But to guard this museum, that takes heart. That takes something the Spanish call *corazón*. And you have it in spades, my friend."

"No one else knows our secret," said Reginald. "We've never accepted another member of the night guards. It's a great honor, and with it comes great rewards."

"And great dental," Gus added.

"Fabulous dental," Cecil assured him.

All three of the old guards smiled wide. Their teeth were gleaming white.

Larry was impressed, but a good dental plan was not enough to convince him to risk his life every single night. Lions, the Huns, that annoying monkey, T-rex, the crazy band of miniatures from the dioramas... The museum was full of danger. Larry didn't need it! He could find new investors for his restaurant. Or maybe he needed to spend more time promoting his invention, The Snapper.

"You know what, guys, I really appreciate the offer, but this job isn't for me," said Larry. "I left my uniform in the office. So long."

As Larry walked out of the museum, he ran straight into his son. Nick was with Don, his soon-to-be stepdad.

"Dad?" asked Nick.

"Hey-hey, buddy! What are you guys doing here?" asked Larry.

"Erica had to be in court early, so I'm taking Mr. Big Stuff to school," Don explained. "He wanted to swing by and see you at the new job."

"Dad, it's so awesome that you're working here," said Nick.

"As a kid, I used to come here and do research on snow days, to make up for the lost school day," Don said.

"That's wonderful, Don," said Larry. He didn't mean it.

"So, Dad, what's your job?" asked Nick.

"Oh, I uh..." Larry didn't want to tell Nick that he quit. Especially since Don was standing there—Don with his job, Don with his gadget-heavy belt... "I'm actually in charge of nocturnal security. I make sure the place runs smoothly at night," Larry said.

"Cool!" said Nick.

Don said, "Hey, Neeko, do you want to take a peek inside? Maybe your dad can give you a quick VIP tour."

"You know what," said Larry. "We're pretty slammed this morning. But, Nicky, I'll take you around soon, deal?"

"Deal," said Nick. "Bye, Dad. Love you."

"Love you too, buddy," said Larry.

As Larry watched Nick walk away, he realized he had to get his job back.

Turning back to the museum, he took a deep breath and headed inside.

CHAPTER 5

All three old guards were standing there, waiting.

"That was quick," said Reginald.

"We thought you'd come around, Larry. Welcome back," said Cecil.

Just then Dr. McPhee ran over and said, "You! New night guard! Come here, now!"

"What's up?" asked Larry.

"Come take a walk with me and I'll show you what's up," said Dr. McPhee. He didn't sound happy. Grabbing Larry by the arm, he dragged him to the diorama room.

Last time there, Larry had been attacked by a bunch of miniatures. Now it looked great. Everything was calm and quiet. Larry didn't know what the problem was.

Not until Dr. McPhee pointed it out. Octavius, the former leader of the Roman Empire, was locked in a stockade in the Old West. Jedediah, the cowboy, looked on. Dr. McPhee carefully lifted Octavius out and put him where he belonged, with the rest of the Roman warriors.

"Why don't you do me the favor of explaining this," said Dr. McPhee.

"I'm guessing that he tried to escape his diorama and accidentally fell into Utah. And that cowboy there knows the Roman dude wants to take over his territory, so he had his posse lock him up," said Larry.

Dr. McPhee narrowed his eyes at Larry. Could this man really not know that the "cowboy" was Jedediah Strong Smith, the famous explorer of the Rocky Mountains? Or was he joking? Either way, Dr. McPhee was not pleased. "This may be funny to you, Mr. Daley, but I won't stand for this type of... of..." Once more, Dr. McPhee couldn't think of the right word.

Larry waited, patiently. It's not like he had anywhere else to be.

"I just won't stand for it!" Dr. McPhee finished, before storming away.

Larry walked back to the main hall, where Cecil was waiting for him.

"Great. I have no idea how to actually keep this job," said Larry.

"You might want to read some books," said Cecil. "Brush up on your history. That helped me when I was starting out."

Cecil patted Larry on the shoulder and then left the room.

Just then, Rebecca walked by. She was leading a tour of schoolchildren.

"This museum was originally dedicated to President Theodore Roosevelt," she explained. "He had a passion for history and believed that the more you knew about the past, the better prepared you were for the present."

Well, if Larry wanted to keep his job, he sure needed to learn about the past. What better way to learn than on a school tour led by the beautiful tour guide? He followed Rebecca and the children.

She led them to the glassed-in display of Lewis and Clark and Sacajawea. "Sacajawea was the Shoshone Indian woman who led Lewis and Clark on their expedition to find the Pacific Ocean. She was a woman of few words. She spoke almost no English. Lewis and Clark wrote that her bravery inspired them to keep heading west. Any questions?"

Larry raised his hand and asked, "Was she deaf?"

"Was she deaf?" Rebecca repeated. She seemed surprised. "Uh, no, she was not."

"Okay," said Larry. "It just seems like she's pretty unresponsive, you know?"

Rebecca was so confused. "Right, that's because she's a statue. Shall we continue?"

Next Rebecca led the tour to the African plains. She pointed to Dexter and said, "Above us, you'll notice the capuchin monkey, a highly intelligent primate known for its loving and generous nature."

Larry thought back to all of Dexter's mischief from the night before. His nose still hurt from when Dexter bit him. Loving and generous, Rebecca had said. "Yeah, right!" Larry couldn't help but blurt out.

"Excuse me?" said Rebecca.

"Sorry," said Larry. "It's nothing."

Once Rebecca and the other kids moved on, Larry pointed to Dexter and whispered, "You are going down!"

Rebecca happened to see this. She was puzzled by Larry's behavior but decided to ignore him. After all, she had a tour to lead. Next, they came to the giant Easter Island head.

"This sculpture comes from Easter Island in the South Pacific," she explained.

"Quick question," said Larry. "Did these dudes ever eat chewing gum?"

The kids laughed. Rebecca had had enough. Who did this guy think he was, interrupting her tour? Disturbing her when she was trying to work and asking ridiculous questions. "Chewing gum was not invented for hundreds of years; however, the inhabitants of Easter Island did offer the statue gifts and fruit as a spiritual offering."

Larry nodded and said, "Copy that."

Rebecca pulled him aside. "This place may be a joke to you," she said. "But I really don't appreciate you making fun of me when I'm doing my job."

"I wasn't making fun of you," said Larry. "I really wanted to know those things."

"Does the Easter Island head chew gum?" she asked.

Larry shrugged. "I clearly had the wrong information."

"Why are you even on this tour?" asked Rebecca.

"I'm going to be here alone in the museum, night after night. I'd like to learn a little more about what I'm guarding," Larry explained. This was the truth. It just wasn't the whole truth, but

Larry wasn't going to get into that. No way would Rebecca believe him.

"Really?" asked Rebecca.

"Yes, and I have a bunch of questions. Can I buy you a cup of coffee or something?" he asked. "Purely an informational meeting, one museum worker to another."

Rebecca checked her watch. "I'll meet you outside in twenty minutes," she said.

Then she turned back to her tour.

When she was finished, she found Larry sitting on the museum steps, waiting.

They got some coffee and walked through Central Park, which was right across the street.

"So you really don't think Sacajawea was hard of hearing?" asked Larry.

"I've been writing my dissertation on her for four years," said Rebecca. "Surely I would have caught that."

"You've been working on one paper for *four years*?" asked Larry.

"Yeah, well, I'm trying to get it right," said Rebecca. "Everyone knows the facts about Sacajawea, but I want to get into her head, figure out what she was really going through."

"Four years," Larry repeated. He shook his head in disbelief. Since he'd never had one job for four months, he couldn't imagine working on one thing for that long.

"Actually, four and a half," Rebecca admitted. "So what's your story? Have you always wanted to be a security guard?"

"No, I've had a million different careers. But I'm divorced. I have a ten-year-old son. I needed a more stable situation."

"Got it. So what can I tell you about the museum?" asked Rebecca.

"I'm interested in the Tablet of Ahkmenrah. What's the deal with that thing?"

"Well, it's like a puzzle," said Rebecca. "The ancient Egyptians believed that if you lined up the pieces in a certain way, it had the power to give life to everything around it."

"So, does that mean there might be a way to line things up and turn it off?" asked Larry.

"Turn it off?" Rebecca repeated.

"Yes, you know. You turn it on and things come to life. You turn it off, they don't. Like an ancient remote control."

Rebecca smiled. Larry asked so many strange questions. She figured he was joking around.

"From what I can make out on the tablet, I haven't come across an 'off' button. But I'll let you know if I do."

"Wait, are you telling me you can read hieroglyphics?" asked Larry.

"A little bit," said Rebecca. "So, what else do you want to know?"

"Attila the Hun—what's going on with that guy?"

"Let's see, he was of Mongolian descent. He..." Rebecca glanced at Larry. "Are you kidding around, Larry? Usually, when I talk about this stuff, people's eyes glaze over."

"No glazing here," Larry promised, shaking his head. "I'm completely unglazed."

After they finished their coffee, Rebecca went back to work. Larry headed toward the bookstore. He needed to be more prepared for his next night of guarding.

He read *The Complete Idiot's Guide to the Middle Ages*, cover to cover. A picture in the book showed four guys attacking a man as Attila looked on, in approval.

Larry read, "Known for their barbaric tactics, the Huns would often tear off the limbs of their helpless victims." He shook his head. "Well, that's encouraging."

Back in his apartment, he gathered some bananas, his hockey equipment, and some of Nick's old baby toys. Larry had a plan.

That night he strolled into the museum. In addition to all of the historical information he could cram into his mind, he also had a bag filled with props. He felt more relaxed than ever. When the museum creatures came to life tonight he'd be ready.

The three old guards walked up to him. "Larry, we just wanted to say, good luck," said Cecil. He shook Larry's hand.

"And good-bye," Reginald added. "We're clocking out for the last time."

"Where's your tie?" asked Gus.

Larry smiled and said, "I thought I'd go open-collared. The tie is kind of tight. And I'm the only one here, I mean, except for..."

Gus took off his own tie and tossed it to Larry. "Noose it up, hot dog!"

"Okay, Gus," said Larry.

"Guy thinks he can walk in here looking like he's going to a sock hop," Gus mumbled.

"Goodbye, Larry," said Cecil. "If you're ever in Boca, look us up."

"You're leaving town?" asked Larry. He was suddenly feeling worried. "I don't know if this is going to work out."

"Smart man like you, you'll be fine," said Reginald.

"If you're a night guard, you wear a tie," said Gus. "You don't go open-collared."

"Will you let it go!" Cecil yelled to Gus. "Come on, Larry, walk us out."

As they headed for the front door, Reginald fell behind. "You fellows go on ahead. I need a moment to myself," he said.

"He's emotional," Cecil explained to Larry. "Lots of memories in this room."

After they left the room, Reginald's kind face hardened. Suddenly the old man seemed sinister.

He reached into Larry's locker and grabbed his house key. Then he pressed it into a wax mold.

When he was sure he had an exact impression, he put the keys away and closed the door.

Clearly Reginald was up to no good. And poor Larry had no idea.

CHAPTER 6

L ater that night, Larry found himself alone
    in the museum once more. All was still
    and quiet.

His first order of business was locking up the
stone coffin. Larry hurried to the Egyptian Hall.
Once there, he slid the key into the hole. The
Plexiglas shield slid down to cover it, and Larry
ran away.

Soon a ghostly voice filled the hall. "Thoth.
Horus. Ra," it said.

Larry turned around slowly. Through the
Plexiglas he saw a flash of light pour out of the
Tablet of Ahkmenrah. It was so bright that for a
few seconds Larry was blinded. As the jackal
guards yawned—alive—Larry locked the gate
and ran.

Back in the main hall, Larry tied T-rex's bone
to a remote-control toy Humvee jeep. T-rex saw
the bone and got excited. As he began to chase it,

Larry grabbed the remote control and steered the jeep away. T-rex went lumbering after it, just as Larry had hoped. He placed a paperweight on the remote control. The car dragged the bone out of sight, with T-rex following close behind.

"Go crazy, big guy," said Larry.

Larry ran to the Easter Island head and said, "Good morning, dum dum."

"Me no dum dum. You dum dum. Dum dum bring gum gum?" asked the statue.

"Yes, I did, fathead. Lots of gum gum." Larry showed the Easter Island head a few packages of Big League Chew. "Open sesame," he said.

The Easter Island head opened his mouth and Larry shoved in lots of gum.

"Mmmm," said the statue.

Hoping that would keep the statue quiet, Larry walked to the Neanderthals. Since they were having so much trouble starting a fire with rocks and sticks, he tossed them a lighter. "Here you go, fellas."

Next he headed to the diorama room. He closed the Mayan diorama, locking them all in. They all screamed and pleaded with him. Then they started throwing blow darts, but it was too late. They were trapped!

On the other side of the room, Octavius had gathered all of his troops. The Romans were using a battering ram to try and break through the wall separating the Romans from the railroad-building area, in Utah.

"Heave! Heave! Heave!" Octavius ordered.

"What are you guys doing?" asked Larry.

"Carthage is in our sights," said Octavius. "We expand or we die. Heave! Heave!"

Just then, Larry heard a commotion from the railroad diorama. Jedediah, the cowboys, and the Irish and Chinese railroad workers were trying to blow up the mountain range separating them from the Romans.

"Octavius, Jedediah! Both of you, get on out here," Larry scolded. "If you guys are gonna be neighbors, you have to learn to get along."

"Over my dead body," said Jedediah.

Octavius crossed his arms over his tiny chest. "Romans do not negotiate," he said.

"You feel like going back to the stockade?" asked Larry.

"Now you're talking," said Jedediah.

"All right, all right, I'm coming out," said Octavius.

Larry helped Octavius and Jedediah out of their dioramas. He sat down. Then he placed each small guy on one of his knees, so they could talk face-to-face.

"I just feel like it's our destiny to sack Carthage, and for whatever reason, they can't understand that," said Octavius.

"For the last time, Toga-boy, we ain't Carthagian," said Jedediah. "We hail from the mighty U.S.A."

"He does have a point, Octavius," said Larry. "Those guys are just trying to live in their own little world over there." He turned to Jedediah and said, "Your turn."

"I got a problem with these Romans eating until they puke. It is disgusting," said Jedediah.

"That vomitorium took us years to build," said Octavius.

"Well, the smell wafts over to our land. It's downright disconcerting," said Jedediah.

"You people eat baked beans three meals a day! You think that makes for an odorous neighbor?" Octavius asked.

"See this is good," said Larry. "We're getting a lot of issues out on the table. You guys seem to pretty much have this under control, so I'm going to take off." Without thinking, Larry stood up. Jedediah and Octavius both slid off his knees. Screaming, they crashed to the floor.

"Oh, sorry fellas," said Larry.

"We're good," Jedediah called.

Larry went to the African Mammals wing, next. He closed the gate and reached for the keys, but couldn't find them. He looked up. Dexter was teasing him through the gate, holding the keys he'd swiped from Larry's belt.

Of course, this was what Larry had planned all along. The keys in Dexter's hands were not the actual museum keys. They were Nicky's old baby toy keys.

"What's that, Dexter?" Larry teased. "You got my keys? Um, guess what, I don't think so, buddy!"

Larry pulled the real keys from his bag and shook them at the mischievous monkey. "Uncle Larry pulled a fast one on you. Those are baby keys for a little baby. Maybe I'll bring you a diaper tomorrow night, baby monkey!"

Dexter was so mad!

After locking up the gate, Larry went to the Hall of American History.

He found Teddy Roosevelt spying on Sacajawea, again.

"Hey, Teddy," said Larry.

Surprised, Teddy dropped his binoculars. "Ah, Lawrence, I knew you'd be back. You look like a man on a mission."

"I'm going to try and talk some sense into the Huns. I'm guessing that you're not going to help me with that."

"Of course not," said Teddy.

Larry pointed to Sacajawea. "You checking her out?" he asked.

"The nerve, dear boy. I'm still hunting that wily woolly. Checking her out? I've never heard of such a thing," said Teddy. He sounded convincing, but Larry knew he was lying.

"It's okay. She's cute," said Larry.

"Why, yes, I suppose she is a handsome woman," said Teddy, looking back at her.

"I wonder what's going on there," said Larry, peering closer. Lewis and Clark were arguing, and Sacajawea's eyes were glassed over. Even though she'd come to life like everything else in the museum, she still seemed sort of lifeless.

Larry knew what the problem was. "You know what, Teddy, she's bored."

"Bored?" asked Teddy. "The world is full of mysteries and delights. A person should never be bored."

"Yeah, but she's stuck in there every night listening to these guys argue over which way to go. It's why my ex-wife used to hate taking road trips with me, because I refused to ask for directions."

"Yes, well, that would be annoying," said Teddy.

Larry pulled a goalie mask out of his bag. "I need to run. Why don't you talk to her?" he suggested.

Teddy blushed. "I wouldn't know what to say."

"You're Teddy Roosevelt. You'll think of something," said Larry. "See you."

Larry put on his hockey mask just in time. A second later, Attila the Hun wacked him in the face. Then he socked him in the stomach with his huge sword. Larry fell to the ground, gasping for air.

One of the Huns grabbed Larry and lifted him up. Soon Larry found himself being carried by four Huns. They ran screaming down the hall.

Christopher Columbus sped around the corner. When he saw what the Huns were doing to Larry he yelled, "Ay-ya-yay!" and ran in the other direction.

When the Huns had Larry where they wanted him, they lowered him to the ground.

Two of them grabbed ahold of his feet and two held his arms.

Larry tried to reason with them. "Guys, I'm sorry I couldn't let you out, but I was just doing my job. Look at the uniform. I'm the night watchman. Trust me, I'm not wearing this thing by choice."

Attila said, "A-goo-goo bigagaga! Bizoo-zoo sagaba!"

Larry wished he spoke Hun. If he did, he'd be able to tell them to stop pulling at his limbs. Maybe they spoke English. It was worth a shot.

"Bad idea!" yelled Larry. "Not the limbs! Do not rip off the limbs!"

The Huns tugged on Larry harder. Just then, they heard a stampede in the distance. As it got louder, they realized it was headed their way. Suddenly, all of the African mammals—lions, hyenas, tigers, elephants, and monkeys—burst into the room.

Startled, the Huns let go of Larry. Larry managed to escape.

Meanwhile, back in the Hall of American History, Teddy decided to take Larry's advice. Or, at least, he tried to. He stood in front of Sacajawea awkwardly.

"I, uh..." Teddy wanted to talk to her but didn't know what to say. "I think I hear that woolly mammoth," he said. "Good-bye."

As he turned and ran away, Sacajawea frowned.

Larry hurried to the African Mammals wing. The gate was wide open. Larry was trying to figure out how that had happened when he saw Dexter. The monkey was holding up the real keys, taunting him.

"Give those back, Dexter," Larry yelled.

Dexter scrambled down the hall.

"You know what, take the keys! I hope you find a way out, you devil monkey!" Larry yelled as he chased Dexter into the diorama room.

Hearing a low rumble, he headed toward the dioramas. The Romans were in an all-out brawl with the cowboys and railroad workers.

"I thought we worked things out," said Larry.

"There's no talking with these simpletons. We must beat them into submission!" yelled Octavius.

"Jed?" asked Larry.

Jedediah said, "We're past words, Laredo." He fired his pistol into the air.

Larry had had enough. "Fine!" he yelled. "You want to kill one another? Be my guest!"

As he stormed away, he smelled smoke coming from somewhere in the museum. Larry dashed toward the smell and saw a fire blazing in the distance.

The Neanderthals danced around the crackling flames. One jumped in, got burned, and screamed. Another set his hair on fire and started grunting happily.

Larry grabbed the fire extinguisher and sprayed the fire. Once the blaze was out, the Neanderthals found themselves covered in thick white foam. They'd never felt this sensation before. They weren't sure what to do. One of them dipped his finger in and tasted it. He liked it.

Another one scooped some up and tossed it at Larry.

"Come on!" said Larry, disgusted.

Dexter darted by and Larry chased after him. Eventually, he managed to get him cornered. Larry tiptoed closer. "There's no way out, Dexter. Now give me the keys."

The monkey shook his head. Larry took another step. "I'm not playing games here," he said.

Larry didn't notice, but one of the Neanderthals was peering out of the open window. Outside, a homeless man was warming his hands on a trash can fire.

The Neanderthal grunted and then dove out the window.

Larry missed the whole thing because he was so intent on getting back his keys. "Nice and easy, Dex. That's right."

As Larry reached for the key ring, Dexter slapped him across the face.

"Ow!" yelled Larry.

Dexter smiled. Larry smacked him back.

Just then, Teddy Roosevelt rounded the corner on his horse. He stopped short and stared in disbelief.

"Good lord, man, what is the matter with you? He is your primate brother!"

Larry said, "Teddy, this guy has been pushing me and pushing me. Every man has a limit."

"Lawrence, you must treat this creature with love and respect. Without him, there would be no us." Teddy Roosevelt held out his hands and looked at Dexter. "May I please have the keys, friend?" he asked.

Dexter smiled and handed the keys to Teddy. Teddy rubbed Dexter's head.

Larry said, "Well, you seem to know what you're doing, Teddy, so I'm going to take a coffee break."

Larry turned around and started to walk away.

"This is no time for a break. The museum is a mess," said Teddy.

"Yes, it is. And I'm not the guy to fix it," Larry said.

"Lawrence, some men are born great. Other men have greatness—"

"I know, Teddy," said Larry. "Other men have greatness thrust upon them. You hit me with that chestnut last night. The thing is, not everyone is great, okay? Some of us are just ordinary."

Just then, Larry heard a pop and then a groan. He ran to the Easter Island head, which was now covered in bubble gum.

"You wanted gum gum, dum dum, you got it!" said Larry as he stormed away.

When he got back to the lobby, Larry sat down and put his feet up on the desk.

Teddy strolled over to him and sat down. "Dear God, man, you've got work to do. The Neanderthals have somehow discovered fire! My friend from Easter Island is smothered in some unholy gunk.

There's a war raging in the diorama room, and look at poor Rexy. He's as quiet as some lap dog!"

Teddy pointed to T-rex. He was lying near his riser, watching as the electronic jeep rammed itself into the wall repeatedly.

"I tried, Teddy." Larry threw his hands up in defeat. "I came back tonight, didn't I?"

"You call that trying?" asked Teddy. "You tried to take the easy way out. You can't shortcut your way to success, young man. You think I built the Panama Canal in a day? Good lord, no. It took years. We fought through snags, pitfalls, and yellow fever, but we kept right on digging."

"Yeah, that was the Panama Canal. This is some freak show of a museum where everything comes to life."

Teddy stood up and patted Larry on the back. "Where is your vision, Lawrence? Perhaps if you could teach the creatures in here how to get along, they wouldn't need to be locked up night after night. Good-bye."

As Teddy walked away, Larry called, "Thank you, Teddy. I have no idea what that actually means, but thank you."

Soon it was the dawn of a new day. Larry had a feeling it was going to be a rotten one. He pulled himself up from the desk. Then he walked through the museum to have one last look at the mess that was made under his watch.

When he walked by the open window, he noticed the Neanderthal who'd escaped. Now he was standing in front of the trash can banging two rocks together. Frustrated, the Neanderthal threw down the rocks and ran away.

Larry noticed that the sun was starting to rise. "Oh no," he cried.

He turned around and ran full speed down the corridor.

Larry sped across the lobby and threw open the front doors. "Wait!" he yelled to the Neanderthal.

The Neanderthal turned around, looked up at the sky, and frowned. It was too late for him. He turned to dust.

Larry was horrified. "Oh no!" he cried.

Turning around, he was relieved to see that all the other creatures were safe and sound and frozen.

He walked up to the statue of Teddy Roosevelt and said, "I know, Teddy. I'm sorry."

CHAPTER 7

L ater that morning, Nick took a couple of his
friends to the museum.

"I took this tour in second grade," one of his
friends complained.

"I'm telling you, my dad is going to hook us
up. He'll show us some cool behind the scenes
stuff," Nick explained.

Just then, Larry rounded the corner. He was
with Dr. McPhee, who was in the middle of listing
everything wrong with the museum that day.

"You put chewing gum all over the precious
Easter Island sculpture. The diorama figures are
scattered on the floor. There's extinguishing foam
in the Neanderthal display!" said Dr. McPhee.

"I was going to clean that up," said Larry.

"What is the matter with you, Mr. Daley? This
is a museum. A place for learning! It's not a
playground for your childhood antics."

Nick and his friends heard the whole thing. One of them said, "I don't think we're getting a tour today."

"Looks like your dad is getting fired, dude," said the other.

Nick didn't know what to say. He watched for a few seconds as his dad tried to explain. Then, embarrassed, he ran out of the museum. His friends followed, feeling bad for poor Nick.

"Dr. McPhee, I..." Larry began.

"What, Mr. Daley? What excuse do you have this time?"

"No excuse," said Larry, hanging his head. "I messed up. I'm sorry."

"If anything, and I mean *anything* is out of place after your shift tomorrow, you're done." Dr. McPhee started to walk away but soon turned back to Larry and said, "Fool me once, Mr. Daley, shame on you. Fool me twice and... and... just don't fool me, again. It makes me very uncomfortable."

He stormed away, leaving poor Larry feeling very confused.

Before he went to work that night, Larry went to his ex-wife's apartment to visit Nick.

When Erica opened the door, she seemed very upset. "What's wrong?" asked Larry.

"Maybe you should ask Nick," said Erica.

Larry walked back to his son's bedroom. Nick sat at his desk studying.

"What's going on, buddy?" said Larry.

Nick looked up from his notebook and said, "You got fired?"

"What are you talking about?" asked Larry. "I didn't get fired."

"I came to the museum this morning. I saw your boss yelling at you."

"Why didn't you say something? Nicky, that guy is a jerk. He doesn't know what he's talking about."

"So you didn't do all that stuff he said you did?" asked Nick.

Larry didn't know what to say. No way was he going to lie to his son. "I... it's more complicated than that."

"No, it's not!" Nick cried. "How come you can never keep a job?"

Larry sighed. "I'm trying, Nicky, but this job, it's... there's a lot going on in that museum. It's hard to explain. It's just... You know what, let me show you."

"What?" asked Nick.

"Come to work with me tonight."

"I can't. I have to study."

Just then, Erica appeared in the doorway and asked, "Can I get a minute with you, Larry?"

Larry followed Erica outside. Both of them spoke in whispers, so Nick wouldn't hear.

"What are you doing?" asked Erica.

"I just want to show him what I do," said Larry.

"Larry, you know I want our son to have a relationship with you, but we've already put him through a divorce, and now he's worried that this job won't work out... I just worry his heart doesn't have room for any more disappointment."

"He won't be disappointed, Erica," Larry promised.

Erica wanted to believe Larry. She looked back and forth between Nick and his dad. She decided to give Larry another chance. Smiling at Nick, she said, "Get your coat, okay, sweetie? You're going with your father."

"Thanks," said Larry. He kissed Erica on the cheek.

"You're very welcome," she said.

"Oh, by the way," said Larry as he headed for the door. "Do you happen to have a ball of twine and a gobstopper?"

Erica didn't, but Larry decided he'd figure something else out. The important thing was, Nick was with him. Larry couldn't wait to show him the magic that happened after sundown.

Nick was just happy to be hanging out with his dad at his dad's job.

As they entered the lobby of the museum, they brushed the snow off their coats.

"You remember the plan, right?" asked Larry.

"I hide in the men's room until everyone leaves, and then you'll get me," said Nick.

Larry nodded. "Check."

Nick went to hide as Larry took a stroll through the museum. He needed to make sure that it was empty.

In the Hall of American History, he found Rebecca.

"You're here late," said Larry. "No big plans for tonight?"

"Yeah, no," said Rebecca as she gathered her things. "I'm not really a big plan person. I prefer hanging out with people who've been dead for two hundred years. It's the live ones that throw me."

"How's the dissertation coming?" asked Larry.

"I'm starting to think you were right. Four years is a long time to spend on one subject," Rebecca said.

"I thought you're into it. You want to go deeper than what's in the history books," Larry said. In fact, he really admired Rebecca for caring about her work so much.

"I do, but I'm stuck. I've pretty much found out everything there is to know about her. So it might be time to put it down, move on to something else. Anyway, I'll let you get to work. Good night, Larry."

Rebecca walked away, looking pretty sad. Larry's gaze moved from Rebecca to the Lewis and Clark and Sacajawea display.

"Hey, wait," he said. "I don't think you should give up on your paper."

"Okay, why?" asked Rebecca.

"Because I can help you. This is going to sound crazy, but there's more to this place than you think."

"What do you mean?" asked Rebecca.

"Everything here comes alive at night."

"Oh, really?" asked Rebecca, raising her eyebrows at Larry. Clearly, she didn't believe a word he said.

"Yes," said Larry. "The T-rex runs around chasing a bone. Teddy Roosevelt rides through the museum hunting a woolly mammoth and spouting weird quotes. Sacajawea sits in her case listening to

94

Lewis and Clark fighting. So, I mean, if you really want to get inside her head, I can hook that up."

"That's cool, Larry. Make fun of a history geek," said Rebecca.

"Rebecca, I'm not making fun," Larry promised.

"The sad thing is, I thought you were as excited by this place as I am." Rebecca walked off in a huff.

Larry watched her go, feeling ridiculous. Oh, well. At least he'd get to show Nick all the wonders of the museum.

Larry headed back to the men's room and called out to Nick. "They're gone. Come on. Hurry up. It's almost sunset."

As Nick stepped out of the bathroom, Larry tried to spin his flashlight like a six-gun, but he dropped it. The flashlight clattered to the floor and rolled away.

Nick raised his eyebrows at his dad. Clearly, he thought the fumble was pretty lame.

"It's tougher than it looks," Larry said.

He hurried Nick through a dark hallway. "Now, in about two minutes, when the sun disappears, everything in this museum is going to come alive. And it's my job to keep them inside until morning."

Nick smirked. "Dad, I might have believed that when I was five. I'm ten now."

"No, man, I'm serious. I have most of the creatures under control, but I want you to stay close to me because there are a few we have to avoid. Don't get too near the monkey, okay? He's evil. And he likes to slap."

"Whatever you say," said Nick, with a sigh. He didn't believe a word his dad told him.

"Have you learned about Attila the Hun in school?" asked Larry.

"Yeah, they call him the Mongolian Marauder."

"Right. He's a bad dude. If we see him, we're going to turn around and run, fast. You got me?"

"Dad, you don't have to make this stuff up to impress me," said Nick.

Larry looked up at the skylight. The last of the rays of light had faded.

"I'm not making it up. Nick, I give you..." Larry spun Nick around and pointed to the gigantic dinosaur. "*Tyrannosaurus rex*!" he cried.

Larry expected T-rex to move, but he didn't. Nothing did.

"Come on, guys," Larry called. "Thor Horus Ra. Let's get it going."

The museum was still and silent.

"One second," said Larry.

He walked over to Teddy Roosevelt and tapped him on the knee. "T.R., you playing one of your jokes?" he whispered. "Rise and shine, buddy. I got my kid here."

"Just stop, okay? I don't believe you," Nick yelled.

"Nick, I'm telling you, when the tablet lights up..." Larry's voice trailed off. He realized what the problem was. "There must be something wrong with it. Come on."

Larry led Nick to the Egyptian Hall. When he shined the light on the wall where the Tablet of Ahkmenrah should have been, he found that it was empty. "It's gone," said Larry.

"What's gone?" asked Nick.

"That, the Tablet of Ahkmenrah. It gives life to everything in the museum. Somebody stole it."

"Uh-huh," said Nick. Not believing, he turned around and walked away. He was tired of watching his dad make a fool of himself.

Larry chased after him. "Nicky, stop! Where are you going?"

"Home," said Nick, as he disappeared down the stairs.

Larry chased after him. When he passed by the window leading to the loading dock, he noticed something strange. Three men were pushing a large crate onto the delivery dock. An old van was parked there. Its back doors were open.

Nick headed out to the same area, but by the time Larry got there, he couldn't see anyone else.

Larry whispered to his son. "Nick!"

"Dad, what's going on here?" asked Nick, stepping out from the shadows.

"That's what I'm trying to figure out." Larry shined the light on the floor and noticed something familiar. "That's my jacket." He lifted it up to reveal the Tablet of Ahkmenrah.

Nick picked up the solid gold tablet. "Whoa!" he said.

"You guys shouldn't be here," said Cecil.

Larry turned around and found all three guards standing there.

"Hey, what are you doing here? Aren't you supposed to be in Florida?" asked Larry.

"I'm afraid not," said Cecil.

"Give us the tablet, son," said Reginald.

"Are you guys robbing the museum?" asked Larry.

"Robbing the museum? We're the night watchmen. Why would we do a thing like that?" asked Cecil.

Larry stared at the tablet. "The pieces are out of whack. That's why nothing came to life," he said.

The old guards shook their heads. "Look, kid, I hate to tell you this, but your dad doesn't even work here anymore. The director fired him today. He couldn't hack it," said Cecil.

Nick looked from the guards to Larry. He seemed so heartbroken. "I thought you said..."

"I did. They're lying, Nick. All you have to do is move that bottom piece to the left. You'll see what I was talking about," said Larry.

"That's museum property, son," said Cecil. "Give it back and we won't tell the cops you were here after hours."

Cecil reached for the tablet. Nick looked at his father. He started to hand it over.

Larry felt like his heart was breaking in half.

Then, suddenly, Nick took it back and pushed the bottom piece into place.

"NOOO!" yelled Cecil.

The tablet began to glow. Just then a ghostly voice called, "Thor. Horus. Ra."

Something stirred from the museum. Many things. But that wasn't all. The guards began to glow. Their bodies trembled. Cecil shook out his bad knee. Reginald raised his cane above his head and stretched. Gus puffed out his chest and cracked his knuckles.

Meanwhile, Nick was getting scared. "Dad?" he asked. His voice sounded shaky.

"It's okay," said Larry.

Suddenly the three men seemed younger, more energetic, not like the old guys they were just a minute before. "Ah, that's much better," said Cecil. "Larry, this would be a great time for your kid to give us the tablet."

Reginald waved his cane, threateningly. Gus curled his fist.

Larry leaned down to his son and said, "Nick, remember what I told you to do if we saw Atilla the Hun?"

"Yup," said Nick.

"Do it now," said Larry.

Suddenly, Nick spun around and dashed off the loading dock and back into the museum. The guards tried to follow, but Larry blocked their path. He stood in front of the door, not letting them through.

"Bad idea, Larry," said Cecil.

Gus approached, holding up his fists. "You want to dance, hot dog? Let's dance."

"Come on, Gus, you're an old man. I don't want to... OOF!!" Just then Gus socked Larry in the nose. Then he kept on hitting him.

"Ow, hey, stop it! Reginald, would you tell him to..." Larry was in too much pain to finish his thought.

Reginald held up his cane and said, "Okay, Gus, that's enough."

"Thank you," said Larry.

Once Gus backed away, Reginald hit Larry in the stomach. Larry doubled over and the guard hit him on the back.

Larry stumbled. Then Cecil approached and started kickboxing him.

He hit him in the face and stomach until Larry was too weak to stand.

"What are you guys doing?" asked Larry as he fell to the ground.

Cecil explained it. "You see, Larry, a few years into the job, the three of us realized that, like everything else in the museum, we got new life at night. Sundown to sunrise, we felt young, again."

"It gave us energy, to boot," said Reginald.

"Exactly. A boost of energy. When this tablet glows, our aches and pains disappear," said Cecil.

"We move around like teenagers," said Reginald. He did a little dance, to demonstrate. "I taught myself the tango."

"We only pee once a night," said Gus.

"We love the nightlife, Larry. So when we found out they were gonna fire us, we knew we had to steal the tablet," said Cecil.

"That's why you hired me?" asked Larry. "It was a setup?"

The three of them nodded.

"We had to find the perfect fall guy and the truth is, my friend, you're a bit of a loser. You move from place to place, job to job," said Cecil.

"Everyone knows you need the money," said Reginald.

"You take all that, plus the precious jewels and things that we stole from here and planted in your apartment, it seems pretty clear you committed the crime." As Cecil turned to leave he said, "Come on, boys, let's find the kid."

Larry could not believe they set him up!

The old guards walked back into the museum. Larry tried to get up but Gus kicked him one last time in the ribs. He fell down in a heap.

Back in the Egyptian Hall, Nick crept around in search of a place to hide.

When he heard the three old guards enter, he froze.

"We know you're in here, kid," Cecil called.

"We don't want to hurt you, son," said Reginald. "We just want the tablet."

Nick crouched behind a jackal guard's leg. It would have been the perfect hiding spot, if the jackal hadn't bent down and put his face right up to Nick's. Scared half to death, Nick screamed and ran away.

He bumped straight into Cecil, who grabbed the tablet. "Thank you very much. We'll take it from here."

"Nick?" asked Larry, limping into the room.

"Ah, Larry, perfect timing," said Cecil. "We were just locking up."

Cecil grabbed Larry and tossed him deep into the hall. Then the three guards walked out, locking the gate behind them.

Larry and Nicky were trapped inside the Egyptian Hall.

CHAPTER 8

Back on the loading dock, Cecil put the tablet in the van. He turned to the other two guards and said, "Let's steal everything we can sell easily. I don't know about you but, I'm planning for a long retirement."

"Miami Beach!" Gus said, pumping his fist in victory.

"Shuffleboard," Reginald yelled happily.

It was a strange view of paradise, but, hey, these guys were pretty old.

Just then Dexter, the monkey, appeared from around the corner. He looked out, saw freedom beyond the van, and liked it. Turning around, he motioned to someone behind him. The woolly mammoth lumbered onto the loading dock, stuck its trunk into the snow, and howled with delight.

He walked further outside. Other museum creatures were escaping, too. Their lives were in danger, but the three old guards didn't care.

Meanwhile, back in the Egyptian Hall, Larry and Nick rattled the cage.

Ahkmenrah screamed and pounded from his coffin.

Nick and Larry heard something from outside. They peered out the window and could hardly believe their eyes. Outside, in Central Park, were a leopard, two zebras, a couple of Eskimos, and the woolly mammoth.

All of the animals were leaving the museum!

"Okay, that's bad," said Larry.

Little did he know, Dexter was at the loading dock, ushering even more creatures out. Vikings and ostriches, alike... the Mayans started to leave, but since they were only wearing tiny loin cloths, they got too cold and headed back into the museum.

"I'm sorry I brought you here, Nicky," said Larry.

"It's okay, Dad," Nick replied.

"No, it's not okay. I screwed this up just like I screwed up every other thing I've ever tried to do. I don't know why I can't—"

Before he finished, Nick said, "Dad, let's talk about this later, okay? Those guys look pretty angry."

Larry noticed that the jackal guards were heading toward them, with spears in their hands.

"Teddy! Teddy!" Larry yelled. "If you're out there, I need you, pal!"

The jackals were almost there when Teddy rode up on his horse. "Did someone call my name?" he asked.

Nick could hardly believe he was staring at the twenty-sixth president of the United States.

"Theodore Roosevelt, at your service," Teddy said to Nick. "You must be Nick. It's an absolute pleasure, my dear boy. I've heard so much about you."

Nick was speechless.

Larry motioned to the jackals. "Teddy, we're in a serious jackal situation."

"Those jackals are merely soldiers, Lawrence. Soldiers follow their leader," Teddy explained.

"That's terrific," said Larry. "But can you get us out of here?"

"For the last time, you must help yourself! This is your moment, Lawrence," said Teddy.

"Save the lecture, Teddy. We're locked in an Egyptian tomb with stone jackals coming to kill us! I need your help. I'm not you, okay? I was never the president of the United States. I don't hunt woolly mammoths. I didn't build the Panama Canal."

"Yes, yes, that's true. I really did do a lot."
Teddy sighed and removed his glasses. "Actually,
I never did any of that. Teddy Roosevelt did. I
was made in a mannequin factory in Poughkeepsie.
I've never killed a wild beast. Or been brave
enough to tell that girl that I love her. But you,
Larry, you cannot quit this time. What are you so
afraid of? Failing? Poppycock. This is your chance
to finish the job, man. To seize the moment of
greatness you've been waiting for."

Larry needed to think, but he didn't have any
time. The jackals were closing in on him and
Nick.

"I'm made of wax, Larry. What are you made
of?" With those final words, Teddy rode away.

The jackals towered over Nick and Larry. They
raised their spears.

"Soldiers follow their leader," Larry mumbled.
"That's helpful, Teddy. He's always spouting these
ridiculous..."

Just then Ahkmenrah let out a horrible scream
from his coffin.

"I'm scared, Dad," said Nick.

"That's it. They follow their leader." Suddenly
Larry knew exactly what to do. All he needed was
to get there in time. "Nicky, follow me."

Nick and Larry ran through the long legs of the jackals. They went up to the stone coffin.

Larry picked up his flashlight and used it to pry off the lid. Then he and Nick shoved it aside with all their might.

The lid slammed to the floor, causing dust to puff up.

Inside was a mummy wrapped in old, dirty linen shrouds.

The jackal guards turned and pointed their swords at Larry and Nick, when suddenly, the mummy began kicking and screaming.

Without the lid, the screams sounded human.

Nick and Larry began unwrapping the mummy.

Once the dust cleared, they found themselves face-to-face with King Ahkmenrah. He was a teenage kid wearing a gold Egyptian skirt.

One piece of linen gagged his mouth.

"I don't really know who you are or what your deal is, but I think these jackal guards will listen to you and I need you to call them off," said Larry.

Ahkmenrah pulled out his gag, coughed, and then yelled, "Khert-neter. Ooom."

Following their leader, the jackals froze.

"It worked!" yelled Nick.

Larry spoke to Ahkmenrah loudly and slowly, in case the kid couldn't speak English. "Thank you so much. My name is Larry. This is my son, Nick. We come in peace."

"No need to yell," said Ahkmenrah, speaking with a clipped British accent. "You would not believe how stuffy it is in there."

"You speak English?" asked Larry.

"Of course," said Ahkmenrah. "I went to Cambridge. I was on display in a lecture hall in the Egyptology Department. I am Ahkmenrah. Fourth king of the fourth king, ruler of the land of my fathers."

"I'm, uh, Larry. This is my son, Nick."

"Hello," said Nick.

"We're from Brooklyn," Larry explained. "Well, I am, and he stays over every other Wednesday."

"Larry, Nick, Guardians of Brooklyn, I am forever in your debt." Ahkmenrah bowed. "No men have been brave enough to open the Tomb of Ahkmenrah. Now, bestow the tablet upon me so that I may assume command of my kingdom."

Ahkmenrah held out his hands and waited.

Nick and Larry looked at each other.

"Yeah, that's going to be a problem," said Larry.

CHAPTER 9

L arry filled Ahkmenrah in. Then the Egyptian ruler ordered one of his jackals to heave a heavy stone against the gate to break it so that they could escape.

"Now where are the thieves?" asked Ahkmenrah, once they were out.

"I don't know," said Larry. "The museum is huge. They could be anywhere."

The three of them walked through the halls, looking around. Everything was in chaos.

A Neanderthal was eating foam from the fire extinguisher. The Civil War soldiers were fighting. Columbus wandered through the halls, lost. T-rex nudged at the electronic car with the bone, but it wouldn't move on its own. The batteries were dead. The Romans and the cowboys were still at war. Neither Jedediah nor Octavius showed any signs of letting up.

Just then, something rumbled in the distance.

"What is that horrific noise?" asked Ahkmenrah, looking around.

"Huns," said Larry.

Suddenly, Attila and his Huns appeared from down the hall.

They charged toward Larry, Nick, and Ahkmenrah.

"Nick, get behind Ahkmenrah," said Larry.

"It's Attila," cried Nick, tugging at his dad's sleeve. "Come on. Let's bail."

"I'm not bailing, Nicky," said Larry. He shook his head, determined like he'd never been determined before.

"But Dad!" cried Nick.

"I'm not bailing," Larry repeated.

Attila ran right up to him and raised his sword.

But Larry stood his ground. "Attila! I don't know why you're so angry with me, but there's a problem in this museum and I'm not going anywhere until we fix it."

"Bigaga goo-goo," Attila roared.

Four Huns grabbed Larry's legs and arms. They were about to pull when Ahkmenrah stepped forward.

"Pardon me, Larry. I speak Hun."

Larry was shocked but happy to step aside as Ahkmenrah said, "I-goo-goo-baga-yaka-mikoo."

Attila replied, "I-za-za ti-koo Larry Daley. Yaga-gee-goo ka-ka-ka!"

Ahkmenrah nodded and turned to Larry. "He says he does not like authority figures. He wants to rip you apart because he feels you are 'the Man.'"

"He thinks I'm 'the Man'?" asked Larry. "I hate 'the Man.' He can run around and maraud all he wants. I just don't want him ripping people apart and trying to escape."

Ahkmenrah turned to Attila and said, "Zi-ga-ga bi-zoo ba-ki-ya."

Attila nodded and said, "Ga-ma-ka me-ga-zoo."

"He says okay and he would like a hug," Ahkmenrah explained.

Larry nodded. Attila embraced him, squeezing so hard he almost crushed the life out of poor Larry.

When he let go, Larry turned to the crowd below. "All right. Now I need everyone to listen up," he said.

The museum creatures ignored Larry.

"Guys, come on," he pleaded.

Suddenly the Easter Island head yelled, "QUIET!"

Everyone stopped what they were doing and looked up at Larry.

"Thank you. This here is King Ahkmenrah. His tablet is what brings you all to life every night, and those old night guards, the guys who ran this place before I came in, they stole it. Now that's a problem because without the tablet, all of this... it'll be over."

Now that the museum creatures understood what was at stake, they were worried.

Larry continued. "So, we need to find those guards and get the tablet back. Jedediah, Octavius, you cover the loading dock. Civil War guys, see if they're on the second floor. Napoléon, you take the Neanderthals to the—"

Just then, Christopher Columbus started screaming at Larry in Italian. Jedediah and Octavius joined in.

"I ain't working with Toga-boy," yelled Jedediah.

"Romans work alone!" Octavius declared.

The Neanderthals shot foam into the air. Jedediah and Octavius began bickering, again. A Confederate soldier shoved a Union one.

Larry was losing them. "That's enough," he shouted. "Jed, Octavius, take away the fact that you were born two thousand years apart and that he eats until he pukes, you guys aren't that different. You're both great leaders. You want to protect your people. Civil War dudes, you guys are *brothers*, for god sakes. You've got to stop fighting one another.

What Larry said made sense. All the museum creatures paid attention.

"What you guys have here, it's as good as it gets," Larry went on. "You're a family. It's my job to protect this family, but I need your help. Now who's with me?"

Everyone raised a hand. From the shadows, Teddy Roosevelt nodded in approval.

Nick gazed up at his dad, amazed and impressed. "What?" asked Larry.

"Nothing," said Nick. He didn't say it, but he was proud of his dad.

"Now let's do this, people! And animals! And Neanderthals!" Larry cheered. When the Civil War soldiers didn't move, Larry added, "And weird, faceless puppets."

Then everyone went their separate ways, excited to work together like they never had before.

A few minutes later, Gus rounded the corner holding handfuls of precious gems. He stopped short when he realized he was staring down the barrels of five muskets held by five Union soldiers. "You got something to say to me?" asked Gus. He only asked because the soldiers had no faces. And with no faces they had no mouths. And with no mouths, they couldn't speak. Gus laughed and said, "I thought so. Now, if you'll excuse me, pillowcase, I've got a van to catch."

Gus tried to head in the other direction. But this time, five Confederate soldiers kept him from moving.

"Oh no," Gus cried.

Back at the other end of the museum, Reginald stole a bag of loot. He was about to bring it to the loading dock when Columbus and the Neanderthals blocked his path.

Reginald waved his cane and said, "Boys, we can do this the easy way or the hard way."

One of the Neanderthals raised his club, which was much bigger than Reginald's cane.

"I guess it's gonna be the hard way," said Reginald, backing away. It was too late. He was caught.

Back on the loading dock, Octavius poked his head around the corner. Once he was sure that the coast was clear, he signaled for Jedediah to join him. Following Jedediah came a stream of tiny diorama people, Romans and railroad workers alike. They jumped off the loading dock down into the snow like pint-sized paratroopers. Working together, they let all of the air out of the van's tires.

After decades of fighting, the diorama people were at peace, helping one another out for the common good.

Of course, it didn't last long.

Within seconds, the Romans and the railroad workers started fighting.

Their leaders were not happy but couldn't stop it. Both Octavius and Jedediah got caught in the middle of yet another battle.

"Save yourself!" yelled Octavius.

"I ain't quitting you," Jedediah replied.

Meanwhile, back inside, Cecil ran down the hall. He had the tablet cradled under his arm like a football. In his other hand he clutched a bag of loot.

He was all ready to go. The only problem was, he couldn't find his friends. "Gus? Reginald?" he called.

Cecil rounded the corner and found himself face-to-face with the enormous blue whale. The whale was not happy. She blasted a strong stream of water from her spout. It hit Cecil in the face and blew him out the door.

Soaking wet and exhausted, Cecil stumbled to the loading dock. He crawled into the van and checked his watch. "Come on, guys, we've got to go," he muttered.

His friends were nowhere to be found. "Ah, the heck with them," Cecil said as he started up the van and gunned the engine. He tried to speed away but didn't move very fast. All four tires on his van were flat.

Still, by the time Larry, Nick, and Ahkmenrah stepped onto the loading dock, the van was gone.

"They got away!" cried Nick. "How are we going to find them?"

"I know someone who can help," said Larry.

Back in the museum, they walked past the diorama room. The tiny Mayans were in the process of tying up Gus and Reginald. Christopher

Columbus and the Neanderthals stood guard, making sure they didn't escape.

"Good job, guys," said Larry.

One of the Mayans gave Larry the thumbs up.

Then Larry, Nick, and Ahkmenrah continued on their way. Larry led them to the Hall of American History.

He grabbed a chair and raised it over his head. "Cover your eyes!" he warned them. Larry hurled the chair at the glass display case. It shattered, setting free Sacajawea, who stepped forward.

"It is very nice to meet you, Larry," she said.

"You, too," said Larry. "Sacajawea, this is Ahkmen... You know what, this is going to take too much time. Sac, Ahk. Ahk, Sac. Sac, Nick. Nick, Sac. Here's the deal. Cecil got away with the tablet and we need you to track him."

Sacajawea nodded and said, "That's what I do. Let us go."

She led them away.

"Oh, man, this is cool," said Nick.

Before they went outside, they headed for the security office in search of warmer clothes. Larry and Nick dug through the lost and found box, grabbing coats, hats, and scarves.

They didn't realize that Lewis and Clark had left the museum. The two explorers had wandered to a bus stop on 81st Street. They checked out their map.

Pretty soon, a bus pulled up and the driver opened up the doors.

"We do beg your pardon, sir," said Lewis. "But we're looking for the Northwest Passage to the Pacific Ocean."

The driver looked them up and down silently. This was New York City. He'd seen weirder. "I can take you as far as Eleventh Avenue. You got a Metrocard?" he asked.

"We have two rabbit pelts and a stick of dried venison," said Clark.

"Fine," said the bus driver.

Lewis and Clark boarded the bus, and the driver closed the doors behind them.

CHAPTER 10

A couple of minutes later, Nick and Larry walked to the loading dock. Nick gestured for Ahkmenrah to follow. He did, wearing moon boots and a powder blue ski jacket. Next, Sacajawea strutted out onto the dock. She was dressed in Uggs and a New Jersey Devils jersey.

"Can you track him?" Larry asked.

Sacajawea stared at the van tracks in the snow and nodded. "He went east, but then lost control and crashed," she said.

"You're amazing," said Larry. "How can you tell all that?"

Sacajawea pointed. Twenty yards away, the van was smashed into the wall.

"The man, he left the wagon and went back..." said Sacajawea as she continued to follow the footprints toward the delivery dock.

"Why would he go back?" wondered Larry, peering into the museum.

Suddenly, the stagecoach came barreling out of the museum, tearing through the snow. Four horses pulled the coach and Cecil was at the reins. It was headed straight toward Sacajawea.

Everyone screamed. The stagecoach was about to run her over when, suddenly, Teddy Roosevelt heroically pushed her out of the way.

Cecil and the horses disappeared in the distance. Sacajawea turned to Teddy. "You saved me," she said.

"You are worth saving, my dear," said Teddy.

He smiled at her and she smiled back. It was a beautiful moment, but it didn't last very long. Teddy looked down. "Oh, I seem to have gotten myself into a bit of a predicament," he said as his entire body split into two pieces. His legs were completely separate from his torso. Luckily, he was made of wax and felt no pain.

Nick looked out toward Central Park. "Dad, he's got the tablet," he said.

"I know. Give me a second. I'll figure something out," said Larry.

Larry wasn't sure of what to do next. He couldn't let Cecil get away. But how was he supposed to catch him when the stagecoach was moving so fast?

Just then, he heard the loud vrooming noise of a car engine. The tiny electric jeep took a massive jump off the edge of the dock. Jedediah waved from the driver's seat. Octavius sat at his side, holding on for dear life. The bone was still attached to the back of the jeep, which is why T-rex followed close behind.

"Yeeh haw!" yelled Jedediah.

The car landed and skidded to a stop by Larry's feet.

"At your service, Gigantour!" yelled Jedediah.

"We saw the evildoer fleeing by chariot. How can we help?" asked Octavius.

The plan came to Larry in a flash. He bent down so Jedediah and Octavius could hear him better. "Okay, here's what we're going to do," he said.

Soon the jeep was tearing through Central Park. T-rex followed, with Nick and Ahkmenrah riding on his back. Larry rode beside them, on Lucky,

Teddy Roosevelt's horse. They were coming closer to Cecil, who started to look worried.

Just then, Cecil yanked on the reins and made a sharp turn.

Jedediah spun the wheel, trying to make the hairpin turn. The jeep skidded dangerously. "I can't hold her!" yelled Jedediah.

Suddenly the car flipped over and over, disappearing down a small embankment. When it landed, it burst into flames. Everyone else stopped and looked on in horror.

"They were so young," said Larry.

"And so little," said Ahkmenrah.

T-rex curled onto the ground, sadly. Then Larry snapped into action. Yes, he was sad, but he still had a museum to save.

"Come on, Lucky! We've got to get this guy."

Larry pressed his heels into the horse's sides, making it break into a fast gallop.

Meanwhile, back at the museum, Sacajawea tried to fix Teddy. She rubbed two sticks together to start a fire. Then she held Teddy's torso over it.

He continued to speak, as if nothing out of the ordinary was happening.

"It was 1909... we were venturing down the Amazon in a teak canoe. Our river guide was a brilliant young pygmy who spoke only by clucking." Teddy clucked his tongue. "Didn't know a word of English! The man simply clucked! Imagine that, Sacajawea!"

Sacajawea shook her head in amazement. Once the wax was soft and melty, she stuck Teddy's torso on top of his legs. He was all back together, again.

It took some time, but Larry finally reached the stagecoach. "Give me the tablet, Cecil!" he yelled.

"Can't do it, friend!" said Cecil.

"All right. Then I'm going to have to take you down." Larry stood on his horse's back. "Okay, Lucky, keep it steady," he whispered.

The horse galloped along the stagecoach. Larry braced himself. Cecil looked concerned as Larry leaped. He soared through the air, like a hero. And then he missed the stagecoach and landed on his face, in the snow-covered ground.

Cecil turned back and grinned. "Not as easy as it looks in the movies, huh, Larry?"

As Cecil turned back around, he gasped in fright. He was speeding toward a chain-link fence.

"WHOA!" he yelled.

The horses skidded to a stop just in time. The sudden stop ripped Cecil out of his seat. He went flying through the air and slammed into the fence.

Larry saw the whole thing from his spot in the snow.

Dazed, Cecil stood up and tried to shake out the pain. No way was he going to give back the tablet, when he was so close to getting away. He grabbed the tablet from the stagecoach. He began to run when, WHAM! A sword handle nailed him in the gut. As Cecil doubled over and tried to catch his breath, he saw Attila the Hun standing over him. Attila wielded his sword. The other Huns stood behind him, looking like they were ready for blood.

Larry walked over. Nick and Ahkmenrah pulled up with T-rex. The four Huns grabbed Cecil by his limbs. They were about to yank him apart.

Cecil flashed Attila a smile. "Attila, how are you doing, friend? It's me, Cecil! Remember, I let you have the run of the place for the past forty years!"

"A-ga-ga bi-goo! Ga-za-ga!" said Attila.

"He would very much like to remove Cecil's arms," Ahkmenrah translated for Larry.

"Let me think about this," said Larry.

"Larry, buddy, good pal" said Cecil. "We can work this out."

"Tell you what. Ahk, ask the Huns to take him back to the museum, and toss him in with his buddies. I have other plans for these guys," said Larry.

Attila shrugged and gestured to the Huns. The Huns hoisted the frightened Cecil above their heads and ran back to the museum.

Just then, Larry noticed the sky. It was beginning to light up with the first rays of sunlight. He had lots of work to do, but not much time. If he didn't get the museum creatures inside before sunrise, they'd all turn to dust.

"Oh no!" said Larry.

"What is it?" asked Ahkmenrah.

"I've got to get you guys back to the museum," he said. "Ahk, can't you yell something and get the creatures back inside?"

"Actually, there is a command written on the tablet that can achieve that goal," said Ahkmenrah. He looked down at his feet, sadly. I just, well..."

"What?" asked Larry.

"I can't read," said Ahkmenrah.

"You speak Hun but you can't read?" asked Larry.

"I really only speak conversational Hun," Ahkmenrah explained. "I'm a king. I always had someone read for me. Plus, I skipped class a lot."

"You and me both, brother," said Larry.

"What are we going to do?" asked Nick.

Larry looked at the tablet. Suddenly, he knew exactly what to do.

Larry led Nick, Attila, and Ahkmenrah to Rebecca's apartment building, which was only a couple blocks from the museum. He stood on the street, underneath her window and peered up. The window was dark. She was probably sound asleep.

Larry picked up a pebble and threw it at her window. That didn't cause a stir so he threw a rock. Still, nothing happened.

Attila said something in Hun and Ahkmenrah translated for Larry. "He says he could burn her out."

"Easy, big guy," said Larry.

Finally, Attila aimed an arrow at the window and shattered it. That sure woke Rebecca.

She poked her head out the window. When she saw Larry, Nick, Ahkmenrah, and Attila the Hun, she didn't know what to think.

"I wasn't making fun of you," Larry said.

"Is this real?" asked Rebecca.

"It's real. And if you want it to stay real, I need your help," said Larry.

Rebecca threw a coat on over her nightgown. Then she hurried downstairs. After Larry quickly explained what he needed, she read the tablet to Ahkmenrah. "Ptah-Seker-Asar. Ptah-Nu."

Ahkmenrah repeated it.

Rebecca said, "Pta-Seker. Ptah-Tatenn. Ahkmernahu."

Ahkmenrah said it, too. "Pta-Seker. Ptah-Tatenn. Ahkmernahu."

Suddenly the tablet started to glow from within.

Larry looked at Rebecca. "Is this it?" he whispered.

Rebecca shrugged. She didn't know, but she sure hoped so.

Suddenly Attila turned around and headed for the museum. T-rex did the same. All of the creatures did.

"It's working!" yelled Nick, jumping up and down.

"Oh, my gosh! That is so cool!" said Rebecca.

"Come on, there's someone I want you to meet," said Larry.

As the sky lightened, everyone headed back to the museum. An amazing parade of animals and ancient creatures marched through Central Park.

Larry and Rebecca stood by the front door, watching. Nick and Teddy checked off the creatures as they entered.

When Teddy approached, Larry said, "Great to see you in one piece. Where's your girlfriend?"

"My girlfriend?" asked Teddy, blushing like no other wax sculpture had ever blushed before. "Please, Lawrence. It's strictly a professional relationship. Two naturalists exchanging ideas, that's all."

"Right," said Larry.

Just then Sacajawea rounded the corner holding Teddy's gun. "I found your gun. You must have dropped it when..."

Rebecca saw Sacajawea and her eyes got wide. "Oh, my gosh!" she said.

Larry said, "Rebecca, this is Sacajawea. Sacajawea, I think Rebecca may have a few questions for you."

Sacajawea bowed to Rebecca. Rebecca was tongue-tied. Finally she blurted out, "You rock. I'm a big fan."

Larry beamed.

Everything was coming back together. He'd saved the museum.

All of the creatures returned to their places—except for Sacajawea, who was busy talking to Rebecca.

"So, is it true you yelled at Lewis and Clark when they wouldn't let you see the Pacific Ocean?" asked Rebecca.

"I had brought them a long way and weathered many hardships to see those great waters. And they would deny me that right? I do not think so," said Sacajawea.

"Right on, sister," said Rebecca. She and Sacajawea high-fived.

Teddy Roosevelt stood watch by the door. "Zebras, check. Neanderthals, check."

Meanwhile, Dexter walked up to Teddy and Larry. Teddy rubbed his head. "Ah, Dexter, how wonderful to see you. Capuchin monkey, check."

Dexter stood there for a moment, then leaped up and slapped Larry in the face.

"Ow! Get in there, now!" yelled Larry.

Teddy Roosevelt looked up, surprised. "Lawrence, have I taught you nothing?"

Larry shrugged. No way was he going to apologize to the monkey.

"All right, well you did good, my boy." Teddy turned back to the list and double-checked the names. "That's everyone."

Larry looked out at the park sadly. "Not everyone, Teddy. We lost a couple of good little men out there today."

"With every great victory, comes great sacrifice," said Teddy.

They nodded and turned to go inside. Just then Nick yelled, "Dad, look!"

Octavius and Jedediah stumbled through the doors. Their faces were scratched and they were covered in soot.

Larry shook his head, surprised but happy that the guys made it back home. Nick smiled. Teddy nodded. T-rex wagged his tail happily.

"Welcome home, boys," said Larry.

Jedediah gave Larry a salute, then hurried to his post in the diorama room.

Larry took one final look outside. Confident that everyone was inside, he closed the museum doors.

Larry and Nick headed to the Egyptian Hall to say good-bye to Ahkmenrah.

"Thank you, Larry and Nick. Will I... see you tomorrow night?" asked Ahkmenrah.

"I hope so," said Larry. Turning around, he looked at the wreck of the museum. He turned to Nick and said, "I am so fired."

As he walked back, he noticed Teddy kissing Sacajawea's hand. Then he let it go and they went to their posts.

"Until tomorrow night, Lawrence," said Teddy.

"No, I think this might be it for me, Teddy. I don't know how I'm going to talk my way out of this one."

"Yes, I see," said Teddy. "Well, if that is indeed true, then, farewell. It has been a pleasure. Your father is a fine man, Nick."

"No, he's a great one," said Nick.

Larry put his arm around his son and led him to the main hall.

"Hey, Teddy?" said Larry, turning back one more time. "Thanks."

But it was too late. Teddy was already frozen in place.

"Maybe McPhee won't even notice," Larry said. Although it was doubtful. The place was a mess.

CHAPTER 11

L ater that day, Larry went to see his boss.
He found Dr. McPhee in his office watching
the news on television. A local reporter was
saying, "Dinosaur prints on the Upper West Side?
That's right! Early this morning, New Yorkers woke
to find a set of *Tyrannosaurus rex* tracks on West
81st Street. And where did they lead? To the
Museum of Natural History, of course."

On another news channel, someone interviewed
the bus driver. "Yes, I'm sure it was Lewis and
Clark. Who else would be looking for the
Northwest Passage? Davy Crockett? Please."

On a third station, a reporter was saying, "Prank?
Publicity stunt? Or is it just a gift to the city from
one of its finest landmarks? The folks at the Museum
of Natural History have really outdone themselves."

When he noticed Larry in his office, Dr.
McPhee turned off the TV and turned around.

"What do you do here at night? How can I possibly explain this?"

If Larry told Dr. McPhee the truth, his boss would think he was crazy. Larry shook his head. "I've got nothing."

Dr. McPhee held out his hand. "Give me your flashlight and your keys. I am personally going to walk you out the door, because if I ever, ever see you in this museum again, I... I mean I... Just don't come back to this museum."

Larry handed over his flashlight and keys.

Dr. McPhee pushed him out into the lobby. They both froze when they saw that the room was packed with people. Schoolkids, businesspeople, and tourists crowded the entryway. The line to get in was so massive Rebecca had to help sell tickets.

Dr. McPhee was shocked. He walked up to the ticket counter and looked at the receipts. They'd sold more tickets than ever before. He shook his head in disbelief. Looking at Larry, he said, "Whatever didn't happen last night... don't let it happen again."

Then he handed Larry back his flashlight and his keys and walked toward the office.

Larry had his job back.

CHAPTER 12

At the next career day, Nick stood in front of his school and announced, "My name is Nick Daley. My career day parent is my dad. He's the night watchman at the Museum of Natural History."

Everyone clapped. Nick was so proud. His dad walked to the front of the class in his uniform.

"Hey, how's it going?" Larry asked. "Nick said it. I'm the night watchman at the Museum of Natural History. And let me tell you, that's when history comes alive."

Nicky watched his dad and beamed. He couldn't be prouder.

That night, Larry walked down a dark, empty hall of the museum. He was looking dapper in his uniform. There was a spring in his step and he whistled.

He opened up the door to find all of the museum creatures getting along. Teddy and Sacajawea rode on Lucky. Columbus and Attila and the Huns played soccer. The Neanderthals were dancing around a sterno lantern as the song "Fire" blared from an iPod.

Reginald and Gus stood in the corner, mopping up extinguishing foam. Cecil looked on.

"It was nice of Larry not to rat us out, but this is ridiculous," said Reginald.

"I'm a night watchman," said Gus. "Not a janitor! I'm not cleaning up after these Neanderthals for the next fifty years."

"I don't know why he can't just keep these creatures locked up," said Reginald.

"Gentlemen," said Cecil. "I'm going to catch some z's. You're doing a great job."

"You ain't going nowhere," said Gus. "Start mopping, hot dog."

As Cecil got to work, Rebecca walked up to Ahkmenrah, who was flipping through some flash cards.

"Okay, King," said Rebecca. "You ready to put those reading lessons to use?"

"I would be glad to, Rebecca," said Ahkmenrah.

Rebecca pulled a huge stack of paper from her bag. "I need you to proofread my dissertation," she said, slamming it down on the desk.

Meanwhile, Christopher Columbus scored a goal on the Hun goalie.

"GOAL!" he screamed.

Just then Jedediah cruised over in the jeep, dragging the bone. Octavius sat in the passenger seat. T-rex chased them. Riding on T-rex's back was Nick.

As Nick passed by, Larry called, "It's getting late, buddy. You ready to go home?"

Nick smiled at his dad. "Nope!" he said.

Larry beamed as he looked around. Not only did he love his job at the Museum of Natural History, he'd also had it for an entire year. This was longer than he'd ever held any job.

Twirling his flashlight, he expertly slid it into its holster. By now, he was an old pro.
Larry snapped, and the flashlight turned off.

It was another perfect ending to another great night at the museum.